Aldilyn Wardwell; Knights Wrath

Adilyn Wardwell, Volume 1

Pluto Hymentact and Sage Ferry

Published by Sage Ferry, 2023.

This is a work of fiction. Similarities to real people, places, or events are entirely coincidental.

ALDILYN WARDWELL; KNIGHTS WRATH

First edition. March 23, 2023.

ISBN: 979-8215124345

Written by Pluto Hymentact and Sage Ferry.

Also by Pluto Hymentact

Adilyn Wardwell
Aldilyn Wardwell; Knights Wrath

Also by Sage Ferry

Adilyn Wardwell
Aldilyn Wardwell; Knights Wrath

1.

I can't help but laugh watching Herschel, he makes jokes as Mr. Walsh tries his best to help me understand the material in front of me. He's not even supposed to be here gesturing and doing impressions from the doorway as I snort giving away his position.

"Mr.Stott don't you have business to attend to?" It always amazes me that my personal tutor could almost see exactly what we were getting up to without even looking.

"C'mon teach, hasn't she been studying enough?" Herschel winks at me and I can feel myself smile involuntarily. My teacher turns around with a deep sigh looking increasingly tired with every moment of the conversation dragging on.

"Mr.Stott the lady has been given strict guidelines of how many hours a week she needs to spend studying, and I have cut those hours into an easy to swallow lesson plan that-" My charismatic friend walks into the room cutting him off.

"Come on! Just this once, you guys're almost done for the day anyway I'm sure leaving a few minutes early ain't gunna make much 'a difference." Mr.Walsh seems almost personally offended by Herchel's butchering of the human language and I can't help but laugh again.

"No. go away." The older man turns around and I watch my good friend stumble back as if he's been physically assaulted.

"You WOUND me! Do you have no heart?! Is black sludge and BOOKS all that pumps through your Veins?!" he yells falling against the wall in a dramatic way as Mr.Walsh ignores him completely. Herschel makes sputtering noises to drive his point home, The older man rolls his eyes looking over as I laugh uncontrollably at my friend and his antics. He glares at my friend and points to the doorway.

"Out. Now. or I will call the estate guards." he threatens with a voice like ice, very different from his usual soft droning while he teaches. Herschel stands and waves at me with a goofy grin before leaving the room swiftly, Mr. Walsh closes the door behind him mumbling about "hooligans" under his breath.

The sophisticated and articulate Mister Sullivan Walsh is one of the brightest men in the country and at such a young age. Barely eleven Years older than my own eighteen and already a top researcher of the kingdom. With sharp eyes as dark and blue as the night sky protected by spindly rounded spectacles. Brown curls adorn his scalp, he runs his hand through the matting around his crown staring at his notes while I watch the clock tick by as slow as it can possibly manage. Mr. Walsh Mumbles to himself while going through his notes frantically,

"It's useless, I've lost my train of thought just..." he stops to take off his eyewear and rub the bridge of his nose.

"Go after that idiot we will study an hour longer than usual tomorrow." he grumbles gathering his things and leaving the room in quite a huff. I stand up the confusion most definitely plastered across my face before Herschel makes his second appearance in the doorway.

"WELL WHO PISSED IN his liquor?" he asks with a dashing smile and a twinkle in his honey brown eyes.

"I believe that would be you" I raise an eyebrow as he bends taking my hand brushing his lips against my knuckles, I rip it away as he straightens.

"And now I must study for an extra hour tomorrow instead of going to my fitting!" I smack him lightly as he chuckles

"So I did you a favor!" he looks triumphant and I can't help smacking him again watching his auburn hair bounce as he fakes an injury.

"My mother is going to have a fit Herschel!" I can't help but laugh at his antics while trying to get my point across.

"Lady Adilyn," he pauses and I know by his deep bow he is going to imitate the proper English he neglected learning as a child.

"My Deepest apologies to you, but it seems as though I did you a favor" he grins and I cross my arms letting out a sigh.

"My Debut is in less than a fortnight I can't be gallivanting around with the help" I smirk walking past him.

"The HELP!" he yells running after me until he is towering over me once again the usual smugness in his expression is wiped clean.

"I ain't the help! Imma House guard that is jus' one heroic escapade short of knighthood." He looks proud of himself.

"THAT AND A FEW BRAIN cells" I chuckle walking around him before he can react but tripping over myself just as I pass him. With a gasp and a flutter of clothing I close my eyes to brace for impact on the marble floors but instead feel a hand on my front. I look up to see Hershcel with a serious look on his face, he barely moved in the commotion but manages to regain my balance for me.

"You should be nicer or I might not always catch you, My lady." he smiles and I get a good look at his Bowtie lips feeling my face flush and my heart jump to my throat.

"I-i'm sorry Herschel you know I didn't mean it" I stutter slightly with the scare and he hums in agreement with my apology.

"O'course Adi" he chuckles letting me go so I can regain my composure.

2

I feel the air leave my body as the maid tightens my corset behind me, my mother pacing while she curses Mr.Walsh

"I can NOT believe that man, I should have him fired for this insolence, the nerve of him, move girl i'll do it!" she huffs replacing the frail maid. The constriction around me worsens as my mother pours her frustrations into the ties behind me.

"Mother..." I ask for her attention with a weak breath as he grumbles more, now about Herschel.

"That boy... I'd bet more than anything it had something to do with him, am I wrong?" her question is rhetorical although I open my lips to answer cut off by her once again.

"I don't see why we must keep him in our house, up at all hours of the night swinging that sword... that *sword*." I cough softly as my insides are squeezed harder,

"Mother!" I yell, taking shallow breaths as she throws the ties of the corset down glaring at me.

"Am I to breathe or just look pretty?" I ask sarcastically and she looks at her work seeing the metal cut into my skin.

"My apologies dearest, perhaps I should take a break" she steps back motioning for the maid to take her place again to loosen the corset.

"You know what we could have done in that extra hour? Do you know?!" I let out a sigh of relief as soon as I could manage to breathe again.

"Yes mother." she sits on a lavish couch, the exhaustion of her rant getting to her as she fans herself

"Your debut is stressful enough without all this... this... " she pinches the bridge of her nose motioning to one of the maids.

"Get me my medication i'm getting a migraine" she says softly as the girl leaves, she comes back with two other girls that hand her a glass of water. The two others lift a crinoline cage over my head until it sets on my waist. The dressmaker, Archer, comes in. A rather spindly man with long and thin fingers. He doesn't speak, holding pins in his mouth with the balls sticking out, his wispy white hair barely moves as he dances around measuring and mumbling to himself about fabrics. His eyes are sunken in and have the far away look of someone who is inside with his work more than outside talking to people.

"Your grace" He says in a high pitched and croaky voice getting my mother's attention, she moves her hand away from her head showing her attention is on him.

"I know you asked for a sage green but I believe a powder blue will pair better with the Lady Wardwell's pale complexion" He eyes me uncomfortably closely.

"Mother must I wear a gown that will be this large?" I ask as maids bring in generous amounts of powder blue satins, silks, and other fancy fabrics.

"Or this extravagant, I'm not a princess" I rest my hands on my head in an effort to take the ache away from holding them up while Archer does his work.

"You wouldn't be in need of such a large or extravagant dress if you didn't look so plain Adilyn" My mother bites at me before taking her fan from next to her to cool herself down.

"I suppose you're right, if only I was blessed with my fathers looks" I retaliate hearing the snap of my mother's fan before she stands.

"Perhaps if that dress is distracting enough people will excuse your tongue" she huffs before leaving the room.

"Dress her in whatever color you want Archer i'm going to lay down" she calls back, I can't help but chuckle at how flushed she got.

After hours of standing and measuring Archer is finally done with me for the day, I stretch as I walk through the halls before feeling large hands grab my waist from behind extracting a gasp from my lungs. Before I can open my mouth to alert a guard, familiar chuckling in my ear eases my mind. I turn to the man behind me, shoving him backwards.

"Herschel you gnat!" I watch him laugh joyously, barely moving despite the push I gave him.

"You gave me a proper fright, what if I had fallen?" I accuse him to which he only grins down at me.

"Well I would 'ave caught chu" he reasons making obvious reference to the previous day's events causing my face to heat up instantly.

"You. are a true scoundrel Mr. Stott" I continue walking, hearing the click of his steps behind me.

"You shouldn't be walkin' around the house all alone anyway." he reasons as I stare at the walls of the house, dreadful yellow stripes the shade of tobacco paired with an eggshell white.

"Dear boy that is why I have you" I can't help but smile to myself when I hear him chuckle.

"Ain't you s'posed to not be alone with a man?" He asks and my heart flutters in my chest causing my steps to falter slightly.

"I am not alone with a man, but with a boy. Were you a gentleman caller and I out in society there may be potential for a scandal, but sense neither of those things are in play here we should be fine" I can't help but sigh deeply and imagine if Herschel were a caller, the flowers he would bring, the things he'd say, the places we'd go, chaperoned of course.

"Lady Wardwell!" I am snapped out of my thoughts by the man in question calling my name.

"Hmm?" I look at his face and he gives me the same cocky smile as always chuckling at my lost composure.

"Got nothin' smart to say now huh Adi?" He asks insinuating a previous quip I must have missed.

"I beg your pardon?" I ask softly and he laughs openly, a hearty and warm sound that travels through my veins like a drug making my head spin.

"You're too cute sometimes, My Lady" he bows down and kisses my knuckles as he does every time he teases me. This time, unlike any time before, I feel blood rush into my face so fast I'm sure my cheeks could be seen beating in rhythm with my pounding heart. I rip my hand away and walk past him quickly making sure to keep my footing as I hear him chuckle before he follows.

3

Herschel only leaves my side when I happen upon my brother's door, I open to find him where he usually is, sitting at his messy desk with papers strewn about. His breathing is heavy and his face flushed.

"My word, what storm has wreaked havoc through here? Your breathing is heavy, are you ill?" I ask him and he shakes his head breathlessly,

"I am not ill sister, I simply mistook your steps for mother's" He places a hand to his chest calming himself.

"You wound me Darius, comparing me to such a woman." I chuckle softly looking around his messy room.

"Don't be hard on mother, she loves you dearly." he flips a page in the book he has on his desk and I lean on the back of his chair scoffing.

"Mother loves you dearly, she loves me in moderation." I sigh deeply hearing his book snap shut.

"Must you be so negative? You know that isn't true" He stands taking the strewn about papers on his desk and placing them in a pile.

"Must you be so dense? I'm not her little boy so she could care less, you should see how eager she is to marry me off to the highest bidder" He scoffs again, bending down for the other papers.

"You must be careful with your tone sister, especially when I become Duke" I roll my eyes curtsying.

"My apologies, Your *grace*" I say sarcastically, straightening back up and rolling my eyes, I can't believe he's taking her side. My chest gets tight as I feel the frustration boil inside of me.

"Why must you be on her side? Do you know what she said to me today? She would never have dreamed of saying such a thing to you." I scoff watching him sit on the very edge of his desk, he crosses his arms shaking his head.

"I am not taking anyone's side here Linny, and yes I did hear but I also heard what you said to her." he tilts his head and I feel my face heat up in shame at the look of disappointment he gives me.

"It is NOT my fault, she started it but of course she didn't tell you that did she?" I can't look at his face, the disappointment would hurt too much.

"When are you going to grow up Adilyn? You're not a child fighting over a doll, it doesn't matter who started it! this Grudge you keep against mother and father is mad" He sighs standing up and I feel like a little girl being scolded, shame making its way through me.

"You must not speak to me about father! The Duke only has time for his favorite child." I glare at my brother as he lets out an irritated sigh.

"You're wrong Linny please see reason" I can't help but groan openly in a very unlady-like fashion.

"Name the last time father has spoken a sentence to me let alone glanced in my direction" I question him and the look on his face turns into exhaustion at this conversation.

"Father is only busy, He isn't going to be around forever. Someday I will be Duke but until then-" I cut him off stamping my foot and letting out a yell of frustration.

"Who KNOWS if you're going to be Duke, with your health record you'll probably be dead before father!" I stop in my tracks instantly regretting my words as I turn to face him.

"Darius, I didn't mean to" he lifts his hand up to stop me, He doesn't look at me sitting back at his desk.

"You have much growing up to do sister, now leave my room please" He says simply, a lump forms in my throat.

"Darius i'm sorry" I say simply but he doesn't look at me, opening his book back up. The atmosphere is dark and angry.

"I told you to leave. Adilyn." He says simply and I can't stand the pang I feel in my chest, I decide to respect his wishes curtsying in front of him.

"As you wish, My Lord." I straighten back up as he ignores me, and I shamefully leave the room.

I rush through the disgusting yellow walls of the dukedom, the lump welling in my throat feels like it's strangling me. I feel like a stupid little girl, scolded by a parent for a temper tantrum. I don't know where i'm going but feel myself bump into someone, I look up to see Mr. Walsh holding an open book looking confused.

"Ad-I mean Lady Wardwell, is something upsetting you?" he asks with more emotion gracing his face than I have ever seen while he teaches. I clear my throat in an attempt to sound normal and not on the verge of tears.

"N-no I'm fine, as you were" I fail miserably, stuttering out a meek sentence in an attempt to brush him off before continuing at a much faster pace. I hike up my skirt so I can attempt to run without toppling over before my tears start to fall. I feel my chest tightening every time I picture the pain on my brother's face, The disappointment in his voice curling in my memory making breathing impossible. I only stop when I can't run any longer leaning against a large tree on the grounds, all I can hear is the huff of my own breath. I feel the warm tears against my cheeks as well as the coldness of rain falling atop my head, I am not sobbing. I can barely see the lake in front of me through the fog, feeling a hand on my shoulder I turn around startled. My teacher looks down at me holding his book over his head to cover himself from the rain, his attempt is in vain as his spectacles are blurry with droplets and his damp curls stick to his forehead.

"My... my lady" he speaks between large breaths bringing to my attention that he must have run after me.

"Something *is* wrong" he says simply, His frames are dangling on the edge of his nose so he can peer into my eyes.

"It's not important... idiotic even." I hate crying in front of people, I feel small so I turn to face away from him.

"Nothing that makes you upset could be Idiotic" he moves his hand from my shoulder to my hand pulling me so I face him again.

"Even the sky weeps as you do, so it *must* be important" I cringe internally when I feel my nose drip.

"I upset my brother." I come clean to him looking away and wiping my face on my sleeve smearing the aforementioned snot rather than cleaning it.

"I made a comment in bad taste about his health... questioned if he'd live to see his dukedom, it was a cheap shot." Mr.Walsh furrows his brows and I feel as though I were a small youth crying over a broken doll.

"Would you allow me to speak frankly Ms. Wardwell?" He asks after a few moments of consideration, I nod my head accordingly and he clears his throat.

"Adilyn, that was a bitchy thing to say, but nothing to cry over" I look up at him and gasp.

"How DARE you call me such a thing!" I push him away from me and turn around but he doesn't leave,

"My apologies but, Tell me why you are truly upset" I cross my arms and sigh deeply, closing my eyes and feeling a headache from the tears.

"My brother and I... we used to be so close, I used to sit in his room with him for hours." I look out at the lake with a deep sigh,

"When he got well I didn't expect things to change but, He came of age and started learning how to be a proper Duke. I love my brother and I feel guilty for wishing such a thing but I do wish he would get ill again sometimes." I close my eyes again tighter to keep any other tears from escaping.

"Of course I don't really wish such a thing, I only mean I wish we were that close again. I feel as if I can't talk to him, we have no time for each other and it's killing me.." My voice falters at the end of my sentence, I place a hand over my mouth before turning around.

"I've messed up everything by saying something so... bitchy." I use Mr.Walsh's words, I don't know how he can hear me over such loud pounding of rain but I trust he can as he nods slowly.

"What is to become of us? When I marry and he inherits, will he ever speak to me again?" I don't know how I could possibly be expecting an answer out of a third party member, but he responds perfectly by pulling me into a hug against his chest. It's awkward as if he's unpracticed but appreciated.

"If you and Lord Wardwell used to be as close as you say, there is no reason you should not be just as close after this spat... or any marriage." He pushed me back to about arm's length.

"I suppose you're right" I chuckle and he bows Lowly not looking me in the eye as he stands back up.

"Should I escort you back to the house? You could become ill in this rain." He looks away from me, the red on his cheeks most likely from the cold of the raindrops.

"I'll be alright, I wish to ponder your words by the lake for a while." I sigh, wiping my eyes on my sleeve.

"As you wish, Good day Lady Wardwell." he bows slightly again and I curtsy back, my skirts completely soaked through.

"And you Mr. Walsh" I smile at him before he walks away, I sit on the bank feeling the mud sully my dress in a way my mother will truly scold me for later.

After a while the tears stop, as well as the rain; I hear footsteps but already know who it is walking behind me.

"What are ya doin' here Adi, you could catch a cold" Herschel asks simply, I turn my head to look at him smiling to put him at ease.

"I'm just relaxing a little." I sigh looking back at the lake, he walks closer offering me his hand.

"You look awful, I was worryin' about chu. I didn' know where you 'ad gone" he speaks softly, his usual joking tone void in the moment.

"I'm fine Herschel." I smile, taking his hand and standing up, he looks at my face closely and I chuckle nervously not reaching his eyes.

"I-i know, my mother is going to have a fit, I probably look atrocious... There's mud all over my dress." I sigh filling the space with noise, him not answering was making me feel awkward and talk more about nothing in particular. I only stop droning on when he cups my cheek looking down at me,

"You're beautiful" he says simply, I feel my face flush instantly. His eyes burn into mine and I fumble over my words.

"I uh.. Huh wa?" I can't wrap my head around his words but I come back to earth when he grabs my hand.

"Adilyn, we grew up together. I know that you're supposed to be like my sister but I can't help it." I'm more and more at a loss as he keeps talking, I almost can't hear him over the sound of my heart pounding in my ears.

"I didn't realize until I couldn't find you, I was terrified and even now I can't get over how radiant you are." I sniff feeling snot still sticking to my face, My blood is turning hotter with every word he says. I feel my breathing pick up as I almost can't focus on what he's saying anymore.

"Adi, I *live* for you, only you." He gets out finally pulling me closer to him and I have no words, I let out a breath I didn't know I had been holding.

"Herschel I.. um" I blush deeply as he brushes hair out of my face, I close my eyes thinking he's going in for a kiss only to feel him pull away. When my eyes open he's walking back to the House, and every part of my body feels weak.

4

Mr. Walsh sits at his desk as I sit in my own seat. He was supposed to start a lesson about fifteen minutes ago. I look down at the book in my hands pretending to read but not wanting to say anything about class. Five more minutes pass and I bite my lip looking up at him as he reads through notes,

"Mr. Walsh?" He looks up when he hears me indicating he was paying attention, no one wants to do school work but I need something to get Herschel off my mind.

"Are we starting soon?" I ask, closing my book and folding my hands in my lap watching him take off his eyewear.

"I saw you walking away from the lake with Mr.Stott the other day, am I to believe you are feeling better?" He asks while cleaning off his glasses with a soft rag, I'm taken aback by his interest in my feelings, unable to find words for a moment. I clear my throat as he replaces the spectacles on his face.

"A bit um... you helped quite a bit. I apologize if I forgot to thank you." He sets down the soft rag he was using a moment ago.

"It's quite alright." he takes another moment of silence, and I am about to ask about class again when he stands rather suddenly.

"I've decided today we will do independent study, you may do this anywhere in the house." He says while walking over and opening the door to the room we are in, It's not exactly a classroom; The room is very open actually, with a desk for Mr.Walsh to sit. There's a large chalkboard in front of a couch I sit on as well as multiple abandoned pieces of furniture and instruments. A small Harpsichord sits in the corner collecting dust, untouched sense Darius became ill as a child, as well as multiple child string instruments I outgrew the larger versions of which I practice in my bedroom. I stand up hesitantly, walking to the door, my dress swaying around me.

"You wish for me to study somewhere else in the house?" I ask, confused and almost unbelieving.

"I wish for you to do what you consider productive, My Lady." He bows and I curse the man internally. If I leave class now I'll surely be found by Herschel, but before I can even think of protesting he is out the door and striding down the hall almost too quickly. I sigh deeply, closing the door behind me and beginning to just wander the halls of the Manor. My brain swims with confused thoughts of Herschel's confession and my heart aches with just the memory of how he looked at me. I shake the thought out of my head quickly before bumping into someone. I look up and see my Darius, he seems genuinely surprised to see me.

"Darius! I-" I stop as he looks away from me pulling the collar of his shirt up to hide his neck.

"Not now Lin." he says simply walking away, my heart aches suddenly and i feel sick thinking he's still upset with me from the other day. I take a deep breath as he disappears down the hallway a familiar maid rushes past me grazing my shoulder before stopping.

"Oh dear! I'm sorry My Lady" she apologizes quickly giving me a shallow curtsy, seeming as if she's in a rush.

"It's fine, Ophelia." I smile at her which she returns gratefully. Her face is flushed and her uniform wrinkled as she tries to smooth out the dark forest green pants all workers in the house wore. She refastened the top button on her frilly shirt and her dark skin glistened with sweat as she breathed heavily.

"Is everything all right?" I can't help but ask, tilting my head at her rushed demeanor.

"Oh! Yes, quite" she smiles, readjusting her cuffs and running a hand through her afro of dark brown curls that sit atop her head otherwise not moving.

"I was just rushing to get a towel because I had spilled... oh!" she realizes something, her emerald eyes widening.

"Oh my! My apologies but I have to leave." she says suddenly curtsying again before running off almost tripping in the process. The girl is strange but I consider her enough of a friend to give her a formal invitation to my Debut party instead of a maid. I'm excited to see her in formal skirts. Ophelia being rather clumsy already will also make things even more interesting, I can't help but chuckle at the thought of it making a mental note to step in if it looks like she needs help. A croaky voice behind me startles me out of my thoughts,

"What are you laughing at my lady?" Archer asks behind me and I place a hand on my chest to calm myself feeling my heart beat out of my chest.

"Oh Archer you scared me, I haven't seen you in a few days." I chuckle at the elderly man, he holds up two pieces of paper I can only see the backs of.

"My partner was ill and I was nursing them." He says simply in his normal croaky voice walking around me and inspecting parts of me, grabbing my arms and making me hold them up.

"My are... they alright?" I hesitate to ask the wellbeing of Archer's spouse so as to not upset him if all was not well.

"Oh yes quite alright by now, I've been meaning to ask your mother if I can bring Elen to your next fitting." He speaks quickly brushing over his personal matters, he stops what he's doing looking up at me with raised bushy eyebrows.

"I-is Ellen your wife?" I ask cautiously, I've never heard the man refer to his spouse by my name, only saying "my partner" and "they". In this I've gathered he's a rather reserved man. He laughs, a forced sound like an old bullfrogs croak escaping his throat.

"Oh no my lady, Ellen is my daughter. I have two you know" He smiles up at me and I can't help feeling surprised by this.

"Oh.. she's your Daughter?" I repeat his words, shock evident in my voice as he nods to me stepping away from my body.

"Carried her myself" He smiles proudly putting his hands on his hips and I'm only raised with more questions.

"Ellen is your age, then Ilean is a few years older... My youngest is Irving, about fifteen." His smile only gets wider as he talks about his children before he thinks for a minute.

"Well... that's not counting the birds." I never dreamed of knowing this much about Archer and my head is slightly swimming at the new information.

"Ellen wants to make dresses." He seems even prouder at this information, his tiny chest puffing out.

"I'm sorry Archer, I just assumed you were too old for children." I say honestly and he laughs again, a sickly giggle like a horse breathing into quicksand.

"Dear girl, I'm no older than your mother!" He smiles and I nod my eyes wide and stare at this alien man.

"I... don't mind if your daughter comes." I finally stay a little eager to see what such a girl with the same genetics as Archer would even look like.

"Perfect" he says simply before walking away, an interesting stride seeming to take too small of steps for his legs.

I try to figure out where Darious was headed while avoiding where I knew Herchel was posted before I passed a place I have not dared to enter in years, but the door to my father's study was open and he was inside. He looked up at me, his eyes shining like a Caribbean sea, surprisingly bright for the soullessness behind them. He brushes a hand through his graying hair showing parts of his scalp through the obvious fake parts. He looks for a moment as if he's trying to remember who I am,

"Wearing a dress like that will get you raped" He says simply before looking back at his paper. I'm taken aback by a sour feeling curling in my stomach making me suddenly self conscious. I see an empty cristal glass on his desk and I can't help wondering about the suspicious object. Just as I'm about to leave he lifts his hand motioning for me to come closer. I look at the ground walking closer to him and hear his papers as he's setting them down.

"Your breasts are rather large aren't they?" he asks simply, I have no answer for I had never considered my breasts let alone that they are a problem. He turns in his chair to look at me closer.

"I've been busy, how many months has it been?" he asks and I play with my hands as he stands towering over me, his gray doesn't mask the once black mane he still sports as he eyes me coldly.

"It's been.. Two years your grace" I struggle to get my words out. My tongue feels thick in my mouth, too heavy to be able to speak properly.

"For that I truly apologize." He apologizes and I meet his eyes finally feeling surprised as he looks down at me.

"If I were around perhaps you wouldn't have gained so much weight." He comments

raising an eyebrow and I feel as if the wind was knocked out of me, like the blunt edge of a sword was forced into my stomach and I struggle to not let out a pained noise as if I was truly struck.

"Beg your pardon?" I spit out suddenly looking up at the man who is my father, shaking in my shoes.

"I'm sure you do, are you dull? I said you've gotten fat." he says again and my mouth goes dry and I feel sick.

"Dearest, I tell you this because I love you and I wish to help you so suitors will find you appealing" he sighs sitting at his desk again and I nod looking at my feet again.

"Are you to stand there silently or thank your father for his honesty and generosity" he asks, picking up a pipe and lighting it as he looks over his papers once more, I curtsy low to the ground for him.

"T-thank you father" I stutter, instantly regretting the action and feeling his glare on me.

"Are you an idiot, speak properly" he says loudly and I wince at his tone as I rise again.

"I'm s-" he cuts me off by putting up his hand, tossing his papers in front of him, his eyes seeming iced over with cruelty.

"Out of my sight girl, I'll be cutting your portions till you're at least a stone lighter, and if that doesn't wonder I'll take breakfast away all together" I nod leaving the room closing the door behind me feeling tears prick the corners of my eyes as I feel my heart pounding. Interactions always put the fear of God in me, I've never known why.

5

I can't stop thinking about what my father said, even as I stand for Archer as he sews the powder blue silks to the curves of my body. I can't help but stare at myself in the mirror, brown eyes and a rounded face framed by long strands of hair that have to be in the dressmaker's way.

"Mother, perhaps you will think of me less plain looking if I were to cut my hair?" I ask, feeling my neck would be much cooler without the abundance of hair upon my head.

"Adilyn I have never said you were plain looking, I have commented on how you believe you are plain looking only to have you lash out at me." I try to recall her wondering which one of us has gone mad, as I distinctly remember standing here just days ago as my mother called me such a thing.

"Perhaps I was wrong, mother my apologies, but my hair-" she cuts me off, flapping her fan across her busum.

"Your hair stays where it is, you are a lady not a maid." she says simply watching Archer do his work.

"It stays pinned up anyways mother it is impractical." I try to reason with her by bargaining with her if I have to.

"Give me just an inch." I ask her and she sighs deeply, closing her eyes and muttering something about her head.

"You would only hate it and fancy yourself a martyr as well as me a villain for letting you." I resist rolling my eyes.

"I am not a child, it is only a haircut." I look at the waves of my hair as they cascade down my shoulders.

"You are a child Adilyn, until you leave this house you are considered a child" she fans herself sending a maid to get her medication.

"It seems these days the doctor can not prescribe enough cocaine for my migraines." I sigh deeply, grateful the topic did not linger on me.

"Perhaps it is the cocaine that causes the migraines." I joke laughing softly as my mother can't help but laugh along with me.

"Perhaps" she chuckles and I feel a pin prick on my leg causing me to gasp suddenly looking down to where the prick came from.

"Sorry..." the timid daughter of the dressmaker says softly to me, never meeting my eyes and I smile at her.

"Stop laughing" Archer says simply from the other side and I nod at him dropping my smile so I can stay still

"It's quite alright Ellen you are just learning after all." I sigh feeling them both pull on the fabric around me.

Strangely, Mr.Walsh suggested we have class in the garden. He isn't teaching though, but sitting, he has arranged a small picnic under a large caeruleum tree, the midnight bark complimentary with the bright blue of the blossoms. The sun shines through the curls atop Mr.Walsh's head as he looks out upon the landscape of the grounds.

"Aren't you supposed to be teaching, Mr.Walsh?" I ask and he groans, picking up his wine and swirling it around in his glass.

"I *loathe* teaching." He says honestly while taking a sip of his glass, I can't help but chuckle.

"Then why do you do it?" I ask, taking a sip of my own wine wincing at the unfamiliar bite of the alcohol hearing him chuckle himself.

"One does not take a request of the Duke lightly." he explains, setting his drink down on the blanket.

"I wish to go to the capital and learn more myself." He explains a wistful look coming over him.

"Is that why you have not married?" I can't stop myself asking before looking at him, seeing his face change into a thoughtful one.

"I am not married because I have not found a woman worth marrying." he looks almost sickened at the thought.

"empty headed debutants giggling at every word I say not understanding any of it" he shakes his head and I stay quiet thinking over his words carefully before he looks over at me.

"Oh! I didn't mean... you obviously aren't an empty headed debutant you have me teaching you." he pats my shoulder not seeming comfortable with more touching than that

"You haven't been doing much teaching today." I tell him looking up at the blossoms on the tree before looking at his shocked expression, he bursts out laughing and I can't help joining him.

"Fine.. you want a teacher here, read this." He reaches over and hands me a book with the title *Histories of Regum*.

"I already know the histories of my own country." I chuckle looking at the book closely, the leather bindings tied on loosely.

"Oh but you have not known history like this! first hand accounts, diaries, letters, articles of war and family bound together in a breathtaking story. It's one of my favorite reads." I smile at him as he talks, looking up at the sky with a wistful look on his face.

"So you are a student of history?" I ask him as I pick up a finger sandwich and smirking to myself.

"I am a student in general. I do not specialize, I'd rather not box myself." he says simply with a deep sigh before taking another sip of his wine.

"Is that what makes you an Ideal teacher? Your accomplishments in all fields" I ask him curious as to how he can hate teaching but came into such a job anyways.

"I'm afraid of that and the many awards I have received for my work in the capital." I understand better now; he isn't happy here, another person who will benefit from my marriage to a man I will barely know. I sigh deeply, a gale blows and I feel the topples of my hair become unbalanced for a moment pulling against my scalp causing me to wince before the wind stops.

"Are you alright?" Mr.Walsh asks and I nod readjusting my tightly curled mane to balance once more.

"Quite." I smile up at him before hearing footsteps, my heart jumps to my throat as I catch a glimpse of Herschel's face at the bottom of the hill as he seems not as happy as his usual self.

"Is t'is what your class 'as become?" he calls to us, smiling in a teasing way, his hand shielding his eyes from the sun. I look over to Mr. Walsh, his mouth pressed into a thin line, the look he had of peacefulness washed away.

"We are busy Mr.Stott" He calls back simply and I can see Herschel's face twist into a smirk.

"Ah, I didn' mean to bother you but you're a 'alf hour o'er your limit." He explains and Mr.Walsh's mouth turns down into a deep frown supposedly at the way Herschel speaks. He takes his pocket watch out and checks the time for himself.

"You're right." he stands bowing deeply to me before straightening back up while readjusting his clothes.

"My lady." he says simply before strolling down the hill not saying a word to me or Herschel simply walking away. Herschel walks up the hill to me offering his hand so I may stand. I take it gratefully and he gives me a warm smile as he watches me stand, I can not think or hear anything he says to me at that moment I can only stare at his face.

"Why do you do that?" I ask him softly and he looks confused, chuckling softly. He brings my hand to his lips brushing them over my knuckles in a soft kiss,

"I beg your pardon?" he speaks softly and I feel blood rush to my face when he looks at me with those eyes of his.

"Why do you speak the way you do? We grew up in the same house, with the same teachers. Why do you speak that way to everyone but then give me such a confession." he looks even more confused knitting his eyebrows together.

"I don't know, I feel as if I can truly be myself with you." he smiles down at me looking around to see if anyone is around before I feel his hand on my waist pulling me closer. My breath hitches and I feel him bury his face into my neck as he hugs me tightly.

"My apologies, I only wished to hold you for a moment." He whispers, his speech completely changed to be the same as everyone else in the house. He leans back still holding my hips but no longer holding me so closely.

"Why do you hide it if you can speak as everyone else does?" I ask him, placing my own hands on his chest and feeling his muscles.

"I guess I don't want to be as everyone else is, I'm not special like you daughter of a duke." He smiles down at me and I blush suddenly burying my face in his chest to hide my embarrassment. I feel his chest shake as he chuckles deeply and I lift my head up to see him as he plays with the top strands of my hair.

"What did you mean... when you said you lived for me." he pushes me away suddenly, his face now covered in red as he holds me at arm's length.

"W-well isn't that self explanatory?" It's my turn to chuckle at him shaking my head. He avoids my eye clearing his throat,

"Oh uh... I just mean, it's a bit hard to say when I'm not in the moment" he scratches the back of his head, and I shrug and pick up my skirts walking past him.

"Alright i'll see you then." he turns around grabbing my hand and I smile at him mockingly watching take a deep breath.

"I mean, I wake up every morning to see your face, my thoughts are occupied only by you, I lay awake at night thinking of you. All I've ever wanted... or ever will want in this world is you." He speaks sincerely and my heart flutters in my chest before sinking deep into my stomach.

"Herschel... I'm debuting in a few days, you know we can't, we shouldn't..." I sigh, turning away from him and looking at the large Duketom.

"I'm so close Adi! Meeting the king, getting a personal recommendation to be knighted and then." He takes my hand holding it to his chest and I feel his heartbeat steady.

"I'll have a title and we can get married, we're already like family, just... don't accept any proposals yet please." I blink in surprise at how forward he is,

"You want to get married?" I ask and he smiles, placing one of his hands on my cheek and I can't help but lean into his touch.

"I would love that more than anything Ms. Adilyn Warwell." he teases and I pull away from him turning around.

"I'm sure my mother is looking for me, I should get going" I smile to myself feeling a blush creep up my neck as I think about what he said.

"I'll walk with you, My lady." he offers me his arm and I take it as we walk down the hill, the wind blows the blossoms on the tree so petals fall softly as we walk.

I take Herschel's arm as we walk into the house, someone suddenly runs into me covering me and themselves with what feels wet and I realize it's water. A coldress runs through my skin as the liquid soaks through the layers of my dress. I look to see Ophelia, her emerald eyes wide as she processes the events. It's normal for such a girl to fall often with her clumsy nature, but before I can ask if she's alright Herschel is already scolding her.

"What's with you? Are you stupid? Or perhaps blind? Can you not see when people are walking right in front of you?" Ophelia's mouth opens and closes frantically trying to find words to respond, she was expecting me to say something first so when a man's voice hit her ears it caught her off guard.

"How about an apology or are you too crippled to speak?" Herschel glares at her, I've never heard his voice at such a harsh tone it's off putting to say the least.

"Herschel, it's clean water, I'm fine." I put a hand on his shoulder and he turns to me, his glare still present before it softens. The look he had not something I will ever want to be on the other end of again.

"Will you fetch me a towel?" I ask and he huffs walking past us both, I see Ophilia's body relax.

"My apologies My lady." she curtsies before picking up the bucket that once held her water I assume is going to be put to use mopping.

"It's quite alright Ophi, although you usually trip over your own feet, running into people isn't like you and yet you've done it twice to me." I watch her face redden in embarrassment hearing the dripping of the water on my clothes as I hold my arms away from myself.

"What's been distracting you, are you alright?" I can't help myself from asking and her face gets redder.

"You could say I've been distracted." she looks away almost wistfully, i feel my head tilting in confusion before she shakes her head clear again. Ophelia has always been in her own world but the way amusement dances in her eyes and she skips through the halls without paying attention to her surroundings is new as well as dangerous.

"I'm sorry My lady I just can't help letting my thoughts wander these days, for I am in love!" she says suddenly and suddenly the explanation snaps into place next to the clues all at once, like glass shattering.

"Ooooh." I can't help but let slip out as she blushes deeply, smiling to herself and looking into the distance again.

"I'm sorry I've just been keeping it to myself for so long I couldn't hold it anymore." she chuckles to herself and I smile slightly envious, her love seems to be attainable, more than a fantasy that will never come to light.

"That's wonderful Ophi, I wish the best to both of you" I smile at her and she giggles openly before sighing contently. I hear footsteps coming and dismiss her before Herschel can scold her more, she disappears around a corner just as he comes into view with a towel. I can't help but feel relieved when I see Herschel although his face looks bitter.

"Where did she go?" He asks brows furrowing at me before he looks down the hall, all traces of Ophelia are gone besides the dampness of the floor and echoes of light footsteps down the hall.

"It's fine, you musnt worry about her." I take his hand before it is ripped away. He turns around with a huff.

"Don't be stupid, if you give one of them even a little bit of leeway they'll all think of you as a joke." I had never heard Herchel speak so harshly to anyone, the tone stung more than the insult and I can't help but shrink away from him shyly. He turns around softening when he sees me.

"Adi I didn't mean... maybe I'm overreacting." he sighs and walks over to give me a hug, I accept it reluctantly laying my head into his chest.

"Are you usually like that?" I ask softly wondering how he acts when i'm not around, he scoffs a little leaning back.

"No, I just know how hard things are for you, you can't trust anyone in this house, they're all two faced." He tilts my head up and I almost lose my breath at his handsome face.

"You can always trust me ok Adi?" He smiles and my heart feels full. I smile back at him and nod.

"I've been thinking, and maybe you should stop talking to people around the Dukedom." he sighs again, turning around to start walking. I'm confused by what he could possibly mean by this.

"Pardon?" I ask softly while walking next to him. He stares forward, he seems almost emotionless.

"Well you can't trust anyone and I don't want rumors to start that could damage your reputation so, maybe stay in your room. Besides, distancing yourself may be a good idea because you won't be talking much when we marry." This confuses me further, although the first part almost makes sense.

"I'm sorry, what?" I ask with disbelief evident in my voice, he chuckles, flashing a grin at me, at that moment I realize it's a joke.

"I don't plan on sharing you much with the public, you're too perfect." He chuckles and I sigh in relief,

"You're truly an oaf" I laugh with him before he stops in front of the ballroom. My father is there, a drink in his hand overlooking preparations. He notices us after a moment and a wide smile spreads across his face.

6

"Ah my son!" my father says joyfully, Herschel looks almost as confused as me. The Duke brings him into a hug slapping his back, a hollow sound rings out through the room.

"Herschel boy! If only I could leave my Dukedom to you, you know you're my favorite, yes?" Herschel laughs nervously, I feel a pang in my chest at this statement.

"Daughter! Herschel is my favorite and I wish to leave everything to him when I die!" he says overdramatically. My father had taken Herschel in for unknown reasons when I was about two, I love Herschel and don't talk to my father much but the jealousy I feel move through me in that moment is undeniable. Herschel isn't even his real son, he has a real son who does everything he can for your affection, and a daughter he doesn't even acknowledge. My chest burns, it hurts and I am angry at myself for being jealous of Herchel for the affections of a man I couldn't care less about. As my father repeats his words multiple times in his drunken stupor, stroking Herchel's hair out of his face, tears welling in his usually cold and distant eyes I can't take it anymore, I feel as if I'll explode if I don't do or say something.

"I..." I say softly Herschel looking at me, my father not noticing I even opened my mouth.

"I feel faint, I'm going to lay down." I sigh, even in his inebriated state my father is too far away for me to stand up to, he's untouchable. I feel as a child would and not like a woman on the cusp of marriage. I walk out of the ballroom, my chest feels heavy like I can't breathe. I walk quickly, my mouth dry; I wish it was Lady like to scream, I walk past a group of girls from the court they're older than me, not by much, most already married.

"My Lady!" one calls out to me, i've seen her around often; Perfect blonde curls frame a symmetrical face caked with light makeup to make her skin appear whiter than it is naturally, i can't help but wonder if this is what i am to become someday.

"The girls and I saw you in the garden with the handsome scholar from the capital. Is he courting you before your debut?" she asks suddenly and my mind flashes with what Herschel said, I can't trust anyone in this house so I must choose my words carefully

"Mr.Walsh Is my teacher, we were having class outside, my... father said it would be better to get fresh air while studying, and it nurtures the mind." I lie a bit hoping the conversation would end.

"Oh the Duke is no one to turn your nose at, if I was his wife I'd be at his side always." she takes out her bright pink fan pretending to swoon. I feel a sigh escape my lips only for her to continue before I can concoct a response.

"Oh and your brother! True he used to be sickly and plain but he's really grown into a man, although I hear he's taken a lover If my husband ever dies." she feigns a swoon and I feel my fists clench. It's always about Darius and how perfect he is.

"What about the guard boy?" another lady speaks from behind and the blonde lets out an excited squeal.

"Oh so rugged! He's probably not the brightest but that would just make him a sweet boy" she fans herself faster and my heart pangs with a new found jealousy.

"You do not talk about Herschel that way, He is not a prize dog for you to pick on, he is smarter than any of you. And Darius is not as great as he seems, I wouldn't know much about the duke, he doesn't speak to me." I breathe heavily and the woman looks slightly taken aback.

"It's just a bit of girl talk, we were trying to include you." she fans herself again turning up her nose at me.

"I do not wish to be a part of your girl talk." I say through clenched teeth glaring at the floor.

"These people you are romanticizing, they have feelings and flaws, they are not always nice and the way you speak about them disgusts me." The feelings I have built inside come crawling out once again and I can't help scolding myself in my head for not being better.

"My brother almost died three times last year alone, he has just gotten his health on track, you are fetishizing the duke because he holds power with no regard towards the duchess, you are making assumptions about a wonderful man's intelligence because you see him as lower than yourself, and you are trying to spread rumors that I am damaged goods because you are jealous of a student teacher relationship." I huff still not raising my eyes from the ground.

"Father's can have favorites, Brothers can be unforgiving, sweet boys can scare you, and teachers can just be teachers now if you will please excuse me." I finally look up at her, her face holding the same disgusted look my mother gives me when I make a mistake while performing my music.

"I am tired, and going to bed." I close my eyes feeling my head pound right behind my eyes, I need to remember not to burst so much, first at my brother then the crying and now this.

"You're correct my lady." I open my eyes surprised by her response, she has returned my glare and leans into me.

"You should consider; Father's can have favorites, just as well as children can disappoint. Brother's can be unforgiving, little girls can get bitchy. Sweet boys can scare you, maybe you deserve to be scared. Consider that if everyone around you is less than ideal, perhaps you are the problem." She stands back up, opening her fan with a crack and then walking back to her group.

I slam my door, my breath being caught in my chest, I feel like fire is in my lungs, a flame that grows with each intake. My mind buzzes wildly, a defining noise. I feel my stomach lerch and my mouth water in the familiar feeling as a shiver runs down my spine. I can not get sick! I shake my head and start hyperventilating

"No no no no NO NO NO!" I cover my mouth, my chest tightens as adrenaline pumps through my veins. Suddenly the door opens. I turn to see Mr.Walsh is on the other side of the door, his face is concerned.

"Mis.. Mister" I try to ask why he's here but can't get the words out, he walks up to me and takes my shoulders.

"Adilyn? Adilyn look at me, you have to recognize you're having an anxiety attack." I feel as if he's distant, his voice echoing in my brain. Although he's right in front of me.

"Adilyn," He says my name, much calmer cupping my cheek before he moves me to sit on my bed, he kneels in front of me and takes my hands.

"You need to focus on my face, and repeat after me." My lungs burn, tired from breathing so hard, I feel sick like I may lose consciousness.

"I am your teacher Adilyn, you have to listen to me." I swallow hard, focusing on his face, his eyes, a deep blue like the night sky.

"My name is Sullivan, I am Twenty Nine, I hate teaching." This confuses me, I have no idea why he's saying such things.

"Repeat it Adi." He says sternly and I can feel tears prick my eyes, My chest burns and my voice cracks but I manage.

"Y-your name is Sullivan, you're twenty nine, and you hate teaching." Every word comes out like metal against metal, speaking feels like a chore, pushing a large rock to a place I do not know the reason for.

"Say it again." He says softer this time and I feel exhausted, I shake my head. I don't want to. I can't breathe so talking is not on my mind.

"Your name is Sullivan, you're twenty nine, and you hate teaching." I can't help but breathe less when I talk.

"Again Adi, focus on the words." Mr.Walsh says and I take a deep breath closing my eyes thinking about the words.

"Your name is Sullivan, you're twenty nine, and you hate teaching. Why must I keep saying this?" I can't help but ask, Mr.Walsh lets out a sigh of relief,

"When you're having an anxiety attack, repeating mantras and focusing on one thing can keep you grounded and calm you down." He looks away with an embarrassed expression on his face.

"At the moment I couldn't think of a real montea so I just said things about myself." he stands and dusts himself off.

"How did you know that would work?" I ask softly, staring at my hands, embarrassed by such an outburst coming out once again.

"I've had my fair share of anxiety attacks My lady." I can feel his smile without looking at him. There are footsteps in the hallway that grow closer until Herschel stands at the door.

"Ay Teach, what... what're ya doin' here?" He asks and I feel heat spread through my cheeks, an older man in my room would look scandalous in any context.

"Leaving." Mr.Walsh says simply walking past Herschel a little too quickly, Herschel watches him leave, I can barely see the tightness in his jaw before he closes the door and rushes to me.

"Are you alright? I couldn't get away from your father. I'm so sorry did he do something?" he asks quickly and I wipe my face,

"No, Herschel, everything is ok." he narrows his eyes as if he doesn't believe me taking my hand.

"I heard yelling in the hall, if he touches you, you tell me alright?" he asks and I shake my head.

"Everything is fine he wouldn't do that." he grabs my face in his hands, almost panicked.

"You don't know that Adi! He could be planning something you can't trust anyone in this entire damn house but me, not your teacher, not your brother you understand that?" He asks and I try to push him away.

"Herschel you're hurting me." he squeezes my face so hard I feel as if my cheeks are about to burst.

"Good then you won't forget, i'll talk to your father about this and he'll take care of it." I try to shake my head.

"Nothing happened Herschel." He scoffs standing up and wiping his hands on his shirt.

"That's just what he wants you to think, I do these things because I care about you Adi, let me take care of it." I keep quiet, he's probably right. I've always been trustworthy. I haven't known Mr.Walsh for more than a year, I nod and he pats my head.

"Good girl, i'll be back later." he says softly before straightening his clothes and walking back out the door leaving it open again.

The day before the debut I stand on a raised platform again while finishing touches are done to my dress by Archer's daughter. My mother fumes on the couch in front of me angered that I had overslept. After Herschel left I layed down and slept for hours, and woke up still exhausted.

"You know how many hours we lost because of you girl?" My mother fans herself quickly huffing in her seat.

"You can't have bags under your eyes for your debut." Her words sound far away, I feel numb. I don't even flinch at the pin pricks Ellen can't help but make while she mends my dress.

"Oh! Sorry... oh! Sorry... Oh! Sorry" she whispers in a high voice almost too soft to hear, overshadowed by mother's ranting.

"I'm sorry mother." My mind feels like it's covered in a wool blanket, like if I stared at the floor for too long I would expel my breakfast, cut in half by my father and forced down my throat by my mother despite not feeling the need to eat. I wish more than anything to go back to sleep, my stomach cramps tightly with the gas made from dairy in my coffee.

"Adilyn, are you even listening to me?" My mother cuts through my thoughts sharply and I come back to reality.

"I'm sorry mother." I say again and she huffs putting her fan away, she reaches over and takes some of her medicine powder disappears from her knuckles.

"You're so quiet today, it's nice, finally a good little girl." she smiles before taking my chin and kissing my cheek.

"Now dearest isn't it beautiful?" She stands me in front of the mirror, I look at myself, my skin seeming sickly under the lights. Dark circles under darker eyes, not the caramel brown of my brother and mother I longed for. Black and soulless staring back at me. I felt like a pig staring at myself despite the extravagant fabric and feathered brown hair falling down my back.

"Mother are... my breasts are too large?" I can't help but ask only to hear her tut softly with a sigh.

"Darling we can fix that with a higher corset, don't worry no one will know until your wedding night and your diet will take care of that." Her words have an encouraging tone but cut deeper in me with each syllable. I sigh deeply, unable to stare at myself for any longer.

"Thank you mother." I say softly

I walk out after changing into my normal dress only to be scooped into the familiar arms of Herschel, he chuckles at my shocked expression.

"Darling if I could kiss you at this moment." he lets me go bending down to kiss my hand softly the way he likes, causing me to laugh.

"I have a place to take you, come with me my wonder" he pulls me back into him his smile causing my breath to get caught, I feel as if i've been punched in the chest by his rugged looks.

"Alright beautiful are you ready?" He asks me while cupping my cheek, his hands are rough and calloused for years of training, large skilled hands so gentle against my skin. My face heats up at his touch and I can't help clasping my hand to his and leaning into his comforting touch.

"Now i'm ready" I feel myself smile back and everything feels right in that moment, He chuckles softly and I feel him press his nose to mine softly before moving quickly his hand in mind dragging me to the east side of the house.

"Then we must make haste my beauty, I am giddy with excitement." He pulls me along and I can't help laughing loudly as he pulls me into the familiar garden under my favorite caeruleum tree, fully in bloom sense the day of the picnic with Mr.Walsh only a few days ago, blue petals falling around me in the most beautiful sight i've ever seen and my heart is full if for just a moment.

"It's quite cliche isn't it?" I can't help asking and Herchel laughs loudly, his eyes seem to twinkle and I feel my breath catch as it does every time I look at his smiling face.

"Adilyn Wardwell... I want to be your savior, your everything, I wish to promise my hand to you and in return ask for your life, your devotion, and your soul." He says taking my hand in his reach into his pocket.

"And I would like to seal that promise, if you'll be so gracious to accept, with this ring." he talks slowly, deliberately before taking out a gold ring with a blood red stone sparkling on the band.

"It isn't fancy for I can't pay for much but I hoped it was to your liking." He smiles at me the same smile he always has.

"Will you please accept it and promise yourself to me?" He asks, I realize I've been quiet this entire time, my mind is buzzing as the wind blows softly, the beginning of the caeruleum tree's fruit is just barely noticeable in the air and I swallow. Every second feels like an eternity and I wish to be caught in this moment until the end of time. I notice every moment I don't answer the grip he has that has moved to my wrist gets tighter. I take deep steady breaths trying to gather my thoughts enough for a coherent answer,

"Herschel..." I look from the ring to him, my heartbeat doubling in pace at the sight of the handsome man I've known my whole life.

"I want nothing more in the world than exactly that." I answer finally, a grin spreads across Herchel's face before he pulls me into him into a tight embrace.

"My god! You're finally mine!" he spins me around before setting me down, slipping the ring on my finger.

"Never take this off, never never never" he almost demands and I can't help but giggle as he kisses up my arm from the ring onward. He smiles up at me, My face surly red from his excitement.

"Say you're mine Adi, please I want to hear you say it." he pulls me close, nuzzling himself into the crook of my neck.

"I'm all yours Herschel." My heart bursts saying the words myself and he moves to look at me.

"Wonderful, just wonderful. Now I can do this." He says quickly and I open my mouth to question him before my lips are captured by his, I'm surprised by his sudden action, feeling his hands move from my waist to my back pushing me impossibly closer. Heat spreads through my body as I return the kiss placing my hands on his chest, his heart much more steady than my own. Herschel pulls away, as he lets go of my body I almost topple over. He unsheathed his dagger from its holster walking to the tree I love so dearly carving our initials into it, I chuckle as I watch him conceal his weapon once again.

"Quite childish aren't you?" I can't help but tease him and he shakes his head with a smile on his face before he turns to me again.

"My apologies but I've always wanted to see our names carved together, just as I've always wanted to hold you like I have only recently." he pulls me close to him again moving me until I feel the newly scared bark along my back.

"Although my Lady... I wish to do so much more now." he stares at me intently licking his lips, his face is flushed and his breathing has picked up a bit as I realize what he's asking of me.

"Herschel I-" I'm cut off by him as he shushes me before his lips attach to my throat kissing down to my bosom. I feel my heart race as heat sparks through my body once more, He stops breathing in deeply.

"I know Adi, I am willing to wait for you but I had to let my needs be heard, you make me feel in such a way I have not felt before but I will keep my composure for you.." He stands dusting off his shirt and brushing his lips on my knuckle again, an innocent smile dances on his lips.

"Till next time, Dearest." He bows and walks back down the hill leaving me to collect myself.

7

Standing in the ballroom I am sweating as my father clings to Herschel, drink in hand and my mother talks to the women of the court. All the way here from the capital where the king lives they've been here for days, swooning over my father and brother alike. I feel out of place, my brother sulking in a corner does not give the room a second glance. The party is not to start until the royal family arrives but after forty five minutes of waiting antsy is not the word to describe the crowd.

Finally the king walks in with his Two daughters and their mother, behind them is Prince James Curtis Richmond the seventh, the Oldest son of the neighboring country and an obvious heartthrob as the women of the court swoon at his porcelain skin, blonde hair and icy blue eyes. King Giles finds my father clapping him on the back of his back while commenting on his alcohol consumption so far. I haven't talked to Herschel alone yet and I have no hope to as the party officially starts, and I am ushered into a room adjacent to the festivities, my mother joins me a moment later.

"Alright Dearest, it's time don't mess anything up, head held high, and keep your skirts from under your feet." She speaks quickly fussing with my hair.

"No part of your life will be as important as this moment, all eyes will be on you; do not mess this up." she lets out a deep sigh before linking her arm with mine, My name is announced as the doors are pulled open. My mother leads me out into the room and all eyes, as promised, were on me. I take a deep breath finally to calm my nerves, my entire body shaking, I truly forget myself feeling sick to my stomach as the look I receive from all around me don't falter.

"One wrong move dearest and it's all over, stand. Tall." my mother mutters through clenched teeth her ironclad smile stuck on her face, I almost feel as if i'd be more comfortable without her. I can feel my chest get tighter as I try to choke down heavy breathes, I feel like I'm out of my body still looking through my own eyes as if I was stuck in my own mind watching the fuzzy vision of myself doing things I can't control. My eyes look up and lock with familiar ones, Midnight blue. The only eyes in the room with even a twitch of concern, My body breathes in involuntarily and words flash through my mind;

"Sullivan is twenty nine, he hates teaching." I focus on him and the words in my mind, as I regain my composure. He nods ever so slightly in my direction before there is clapping around me, I curtsy to the crowd making sure to breathe evenly before standing again as the group disperses to the rest of the room's festivities, and my mother leaves my side. I see a glimpse of Herschel as he is ushered to meet the oldest princess Odette, her dark skin matches her fathers almost exactly. Inky black hair spills in tight curls down her back and shoulders, Dark chocolate eyes sparkle as Herschel bows, takes her hand and brushes his lips against her knuckles.

"Wine?" a man offers me, an obvious suiter, younger than me by no more than half a year but looking like a child still.

"N-no thank you." I step back bumping into the opposite kind of man easily eight and forty if one were to guess his age.

"Your mother says you like to study, I don't have much use for a smart girl but my estate has a large library." he offers large yellowing teeth peeking through his lips. I peek back at the princess and Herschel, adorned in a brilliant irish purple dress she takes his offered hand, they stroll out of my sight and before I can follow them I am pulled by my mother in the opposite direction.

"Your majesty, have you met the girl of the honor?" She pushes me infront of her until I almost collide with the young handsome prince.

"I have not, although I see where the lady gets her stunning good looks." Prince James, *The* prince of Cantus was looking at me rather fondly. Words get caught in my mouth only loosened when my mother gives me a push causing me to stumble into a curtsy.

"Y-your Majesty." I curse myself for stuttering, closing my eyes as I hear him chuckle softly.

"That was quite an entrance you made, dare I say there was not one young man in the hall who did not desire you at that moment." My cheeks flush as I stand pressing a gloved hand to my cheek well aware of my corset.

"You flatter me, your Highness." I say and He gives me a friendly and genuine smile, his eyes meeting mine.

"You may call me James if you see it fit my lady, that is; If I may call you Adilyn?" My mother makes a sort of 'hoot' noise from behind me and I swallow all of my saliva at once.

"I could not possibly, Your Majesty." I lower my gaze to show respect and hear his chuckle ring out once again.

"My Lady I insist, just as I insist on your next dance." He offers his hand to me and my mother leans forward answering in my stead.

"She would be Honored to the highest degree your Majesty." she smiles before looking expectantly at me, I hesitantly take his hand as he leads me to the dancefloor. We start to dance along with other suitors going after their partners, the women delicate and obedient, the men charming and flirtatious. I feel the Prince grab onto my hips as he speaks close enough for only me to hear.

"You seemed truly terrified with all those eyes on you, are you feeling well now?" He asks and I lie with a smile.

"Quite, thank you, your... I mean James." I respond and he chuckles softly causing my face to heat from the embarrassment,

"You don't need to fear me my Lady, I simply wanted to offer an escape from your hovering Matriarch. I am betrothed already you see, you simply looked as if you needed a friend." He explains and I let out a relieved sigh.

"Well I thank you for your hospitality, your majesty. Are congratulations in order?" I ask and he laughs out loud at my change in attitude,

"Not necessary Adilyn for my heart belongs to a stable boy, as Odette's is not yet captured especially by me." He says rather joyfully and I can't help snicker at his words.

"So she is aware of your situation?" I ask after centering myself, He lets out a content sigh spinning me on the dance floor.

"She is, I only trust you with such information because I sense we are the same. You are not here for yourself, yes?" The dashing man smiles at me and I blush thinking of Herschel somewhere in the very room we were dancing in.

"I...i suppose you could say that" I chuckle looking away from his knowing eyes the fact he could pin me so easily made me nervous beyond belief.

"I must say... I would have never pegged you to go after an older man" He smirks and my eyebrows furrowed in confusion.

"Herschel is the same age as my brother." I look up and the prince whose face mirrors my confusion,

"This Hurschel looks at least thirty he must not take good care of himself." James looks over my shoulder as we dance and my head whips around excited to see my love, instead my eyes land on Mr.Walsh, my confusion only increases at this point.

"That's Mr.Walsh, He's only my tutor why would you believe he was Herschel or had any interest in me." Prince James lets go of me as the song ends.

"My apologies, I only thought he was your beloved from the way he looked at you when you made your entrance, dare I say you were... radiant" he chuckles as he walks me back to my mother, Her face is jubilant at the thought I could have possibly charmed a Prince. James bows to me and my mother before flashing his dazzling smile again.

"It was wonderful meeting you Lady Wardwell... Your grace." He nods to my mother who giggles while fanning her face. I curtsy in return as he walks away and my mother takes my arm.

"My dearest, how thrilling!" she says loudly while laughing before running to the other mothers to brag. I let out a sigh of short-lived relief, before I feel another presence walking to me.

"My Lady." A familiar voice greets me and I smile at Mr.Walsh grateful it was only him. He seems to be strung out himself, minor sweat beads collect on his brow.

"There sure are a large amount of people here..." he tries to engage in small talk and I can't help but let out a sympathetic chuckle at his nerves due to the large group.

"Lord Sullivan walsh?" I ask and the usually collected man swallows hard, dabbing his forehead with a handkerchief.

"Uh... yes my lady?" he asks and I smile at him, he seems so approachable in this state.

"Are you alright?" I ask, teasing him only a little before the man nods wildey stuffing the handkerchief back into his pocket.

"Yes! Yes i'm quite alright I just... what does one usually do with their hands at large parties?" He asks, looking at the crowd rather than myself, His hands hang loosely in front of him rather humorously as he complains about the heat in the room as well as the volume.

"One could dance?" I suggest and his face pails from the word alone, his stuttering getting worse.

"I don't wish to be stared at while on the dancefloor." He says softly and I laugh again looking at all the people talking amongst themselves.

"How about we get some air on the balcony then?" I ask, Mr.Walsh doesn't seem to hear me so I take matters into my own hands gripping his arm and wading him through the many people. I make it to the balcony with the nervous man only to stop in my tracks while looking out. It's there where Herschel stands with Princess Odette, I am not close enough to hear what is being said but I see the interaction clear as day, lit by the brilliant lights of the party. Herschel smiles at the girl, his charismatic charm shining through like always as he takes her hand. The smile drops instantly and he takes her hand softly saying something while looking at the ground almost as if he were ashamed, He brings her hand to his face brushing her knuckles against his lips softly. I clutch my own hand to my chest and gasp before the Princess's face takes on an empathetic expression, she walks closer to Herschel cupping his face. My heart beats wildly in my chest and I feel as if I can't breathe seeing the man I love lean in until his lips touch the Princess's in a soft kiss. I watch him grab her waist and pull her into him, I feel sick as I step back and bump into Mr.Walsh who I had forgotten was even there. They keep kissing as her hands lace into his hair, it's such a delicate and romantic embrace. There's a passion in that kiss that i've never seen and it makes me feel like my insides are being ripped apart as I can do anything in the world but manage to rip my eyes away from the terrifying display that no one else seems to notice. I feel a hand on my shoulder causing my consciousness to rip back to reality when I look up at Mr.Walsh, His nervous gaze is gone and is instead replaced by confused sympathy.

"Are you.." He can't finish his sentence before I feel my eyes start to water, I reach my sleeves up to try and wipe my eyes before remembering the gobs of makeup my mother had slapped on me.

"Damn.." I say softly looking at the sleeve of my dress and the substance from my face smeared onto it, I start to walk out of the ballroom before Mr.Walsh takes my hand.

"My lady, you can't leave your own party." He tries to warn me and I swallow the strangling lump forming in my throat.

"Oh look around Sullivan! This isn't *MY* party, no one is even paying atten to me." He's taken aback by both my harsh words and the familiarity before he turns to look at the crowd, all talking amongst themselves. Dozens of girls dressed in vibrant colors claiming to be "the lady of the hour" in a desperate attempt to appeal to men of higher standing. Mr.Walsh looks back to me before offering his arm to escort me out of the ball room, I accept hastley walking out of the room where I can manage to finally catch my breath. I don't even have time to think let alone talk as I turn back to my teacher before I am pulled into him. Mr.Walsh wraps his arms around me tightly in a gesture more intimate then I had ever seen him be with a human being before, He doesn't say anything he just holds me for I don't know how long. My face pressed against his broad chest, the smell of dust tickles my nose. He must not go to parties often, the suit he's wearing looked quite unused from a far but being so close only confirmed my suspicions. When he finally does let go, I feel as if I'm at a standstill. My whole body is dazed until I look up and see Mr.Walsh with a deep red blush on his face as he looks down at me.

"A-are you ok?" I ask softly and he nods while clearing his throat as well as taking out a handkerchief to wipe some sweat from his face.

"Shall we head back then?" He asks not looking at me and I feel my heart squeeze in my chest just thinking about it. I shake my head quickly knowing if I'm not in the ballroom no one will notice anyway, especially not Herschel at this moment.

"How about we go for a walk..." He trails off his face looking as if he were debating his next words carefully.

"Outside?" He finishes and I take a deep breath in slowly before letting it back out in an attempt to calm myself.

"Under the caeruleum tee like.. Like before" He suggests softly speaking as not to overwhelm me again. I nod slowly, wiping my face again, no longer caring about the makeup any more.

After making it to the caeruleum tree I spot the initials carved there, my breath hitches and I turn around, Mr.Walsh spots the same thing despite how dark the grounds of the Duketom are. I shiver slightly as the wind blows before I smell the same dust smell as before when Mr.Walsh's suit jacket is placed on my shoulders, this action is followed by a large sigh before I am pulled into another hug.

"You know if you caught a cold I would never be able to forgive myself." He chuckles softly and my mind drifts back to the prince and what he said about the way Mr.Walsh couldn't take his eyes off me when I was walking into the ballroom at the beginning of the night. My eyes drift back to the ring on my finger, the one Herchel gave me earlier that very day. I can't bring myself to take it off just yet, I'm surprised when I hear a voice and Mr.Walsh's arms fall from around me.

I look up to see a familiar silhouette running towards us, It was Herschel. It was hard to notice when he was attached to the Princess but he was dressed in his formal guards uniform which included epaulets and a sword.

"Ady what the hell?!" He yells as he makes his way to us, Mr.Walsh steps in front of me blocking his reach.

"Get out of my way you creep" Herschel glares at Mr.Walsh as he crosses his arms standing his ground.

"Ah so I see you do know proper english then Mr.Stott" My teacher says simply and Herschel Grits his teeth at his acknowledgment of Hershel's speech change.

"Get away from her!" Herschel yells and I can't help but zone out in that moment, wondering why I don't stick up for myself and not just let Sullivan or any other man come to my rescue, before I can think much more on the fact I realize Herschel has taken out his sword and was pointing it at the other man in front of me. I make my way in front of Mr.Walsh quickly coming to the end of the broad sword myself. I have seen Herschel train through the window of the house while studying in the library and I know exactly how skilled he is with each weapon he owns and carries of course his broad sword is his favored and most skilled weapon choice.

"What did he do to you?" He asks not lowering his sword from my chin and I can find the courage to glare back at him the way he is me.

"Nothing Herschel" I put my hands up slowly and he stares fiercely between me and Mr.Walsh with a fierce glare he's breathing heavily.

"Lair!" He yells like a dog barking, loud and sharp in a way that rattles my brain and causes me to get dizzy for half a second, his tone and demeanor is familiar in a way I can't place that shakes me to my core.

"I'll kill him Adilyn I swear to god." I can't figure out how to deescalate the situation. Something isn't right.

"How.. did you know where we were?" I ask softly and he huffs like a wild bull ready to charge at the right word.

"The Duchess asked me to look for you after she saw you leave. You have been gone for over twenty minuets do you know what people think you are doing, Adi? How could you? With... with him?" Mr.Walsh snorts in disbelief.

"How could she? Hypocrisy at its finest." He rolls his eyes until the sword is pointed back in his face.

"Teach I swear to god if you don't shut up I will gut you." I move his sword down feeling anger boil inside me,

"How could I? Herschel, you were kissing the princess! You have no room to talk to me in such a way." My words come out more hurt than angry and I watch Herschel's face shift from anger to confusion.

"You... you saw that?" he asks, lowering his sword and I feel the pressure of tears brimming behind my eyes.

"Of course! You.. you were doing it out in the open, you know she's betrothed yes?" I ask, crossing my arms as I hear him put his sword away.

"Adi... can we talk somewhere more private?" He asks and Mr.Walsh answers for me by taking his jacket off my shoulders.

"No need, I'll leave you two." He walks towards the house just happy to not be held up at sword point anymore.

The air is still as Herschel and I stand in silence for what feels like forever, He doesn't look at me instead keeping steady eye contact with the ground.

"I'm sorry" he says finally and I'm taken off guard that he doesn't try to explain himself.

"For the princess and.. For teach back there and the princess." he scratches the back of his head nervously. I feel my chest swell with anger.

"You're sorry? How could you only say you're sorry?" I ask, holding back tears that beg to be let go, I won't cry this time. I feel the wind blow and can't help but shudder, Herschel sighs deeply.

"Adi you have to believe me, I only did it because I saw you dancing with the prince you have to forgive me."

I roll my eyes crossing my arm, I can't believe he would pull out such a pitiful excuse. I sigh looking up at him,

"The prince is betrothed to your dear Princess Odette, my mother made me dance with him." I huff and he takes one of my hands.

"I know that the Princess told me honestly Adi I would never have done such a thing if I had known you MUST believe me." Desperation rings through his voice as he presses my hand to his chest with an earnest look on his face.

"My dearest Adilyn, you can trust me, I am the only man you can trust, remember? You can't trust that teacher infecting you and... touching you." I pull away from him at this point, confusion etched on my face.

"He never touched me, Herschel." I say softly and Herschel walks closer, looking concerned.

"Adi I *saw* him touching you, trying to poison such innocence. Honestly you have no choice but to forgive me since your virtue is now in question you have no choice but to forgive me, Adilyn I'll save you." He falls to his knees hugging my skirts, and my heart breaks for him. I know he speaks the truth, no one has ever loved me as Herschel has.

"Yes Herschel... I forgive you." I hear myself say softly although I can't recognize my own voice anymore as I stare into the distance, past the Dukedom, Past the hills. I see the stars winking down at me mischievously. I don't regain myself as I am ushered back into the ballroom, the rest of the world is muffled and I feel like a ghost in my own life as the party bustles and Herschel tells my father of Mr.Walsh's "Transgressions." The man in question is not instantly banished for that would be too much drama, My father brings the story to the king. The king commemorates Herschel and makes plans to knight him as he's always wanted. My mother calls me a whore and screams about how i'll never be married until Herschel says he'll sacrifice himself for my benefit. My father commemorates him and plans to give us the House in Cantus after the wedding. It's not until that night when I am left alone in my bed that I am finally able to regain myself and take liberties with everything that happened, the day washing over me like a freezing wave and I go to sleep that night feeling quite sick.

8

I can't help but glance nervously at Herschel as he stands in the doorway of the room. As a way to not raise suspicion or cause rumors in the capital, Mr.Wardwell wasn't instantly fired or incarcerated. Herschel told my father he had found my teacher with his hands on me under my dress, groping me as I cried for him to stop. I tried to correct him but was talked over by the sea of outrage that was my father and the king. Suddenly I couldn't find my voice any longer, so here I sit as Mr.Walsh teaches in monotone, not looking in my direction. I've sat in this space many times through the year, there is no laughter now, the only face my now fiancé gives is a cold stare as he stands with his arms crossed.

I don't concentrate on the lesson, everything seems far away. The world is so hot and muggy even despite the weather getting colder as the summer races closer to its end with every passing day. Herschel steps through the doorway stopping his staring.

"This is over" he says simply and Mr.Walsh places his book down, brows furrowed in confusion.

"We have twenty minuets left.." He reasons and Herschel readjusts his new official knights uniform, he presses his mouth into a thin line.

"That doesn't matter to me, she's learned enough." He dusts off his shoulder standing tall and superior compared to the older man.

"Adilyn, come with me." He says simply pulling my chair out while I'm still in it, Mr.Walsh opens his mouth to say something but decides not to when the other man glares at him. I stand slowly before my waist is captured in familiar strong hands and I'm pulled into Herschel's chest, he rests his head in the crook of my neck breathing deeply for a moment. I look over and see Mr. Walsh roll his eyes before picking his book back up. After only a moment Herschel escorts me out of the room.

"How am I supposed to learn if you keep taking me out of class?" I can't help hearing Herschel chuckle, a hollow sound compared to the laughter I'm used to almost fake.

"Adi, you don't need to learn anymore, you're engaged to me so you don't need to impress any suitors." He smiles before his expression darkens for a moment,

"Besides I can't stand that man looking at you for even a moment, so forgive me if I wish to have you to myself before I take you to see your mother." He takes my hand and bends down pressing his lips to my knuckles, a memory of Princess Odette's smiling face flashes through my mind and I swear I can hear her giggle through the halls despite her returning home a week ago after Herschel was Knighted. I feel myself wince slightly before being spun by my promised.

"I am ecstatic and enchanted that you are mine, Adilyn Wardwell." Herschel brings me closer to him, pressing our bodies together almost uncomfortably tight.

"Say it for me won't you? Say you're mine Lady Wardwell?" he asks almost desperately and I feel my mouth going dry. Before I can answer him, footsteps interrupt us as Ophelia rounds the corner.

"My lady!" she calls and Herschel growls in annoyance turning to the girl who almost trips when she sees his face.

"How dare you interrupt the lady? What gives you that right? I should strike you down where you stand!" He yells suddenly and something about it is so familiar it shakes me to my core. Ophelia swallows hard, she looks as if she's been crying, she shudders as Herschel continues to yell at the girl,

"Herschel maybe you should..." he silences me with a glare and I feel powerless once again.

"Stay out of this!" He says simply, Ophelia's voice is sheepish as she talks next, almost sounding on the verge of tears.

"F-forgive me my lady b-but the lord wardwell is calling for you…" she says softly and I am overcome with surprise, my brother has not talked to me in almost a month, let alone called on me.

"I will go with you." Herschel says matter of factly and I shake my head, I don't know the reason my brother wishes to speak with me but I can only hope it is to finally accept my apology.

"No Herschel.. He only called me and I'd rather not make him feel as if I don't trust him." I say softly and Herschel's brows furrowed.

"I told you before Adi you can only trust me." he reasons and I shake my head again, walking to Ophelia's side.

"Until we are married I am still above you despite your new status Herschel don't forget yourself." I speak softly without much confidence. Herschel clenches his fists looking away from me speaking through fitted teeth.

"I will escort you rather than *Her*" He glares at Ophelia before pushing her away and grabbing my waist again.

I walk to my brother's room, a room I've seen a hundred times before, a place that once served as a sort of sanctuary was now so foreign to me. Hopefully the comfort of the large dark wooden door would return to me, Large intricate carvings in the marble, totems put there when my brother was young and sick. The boar signaling good health, grape vines meaning growth, butterflies for good luck. I wanted to learn stone carving or even just drawing when I was young. I was told as a woman my hands were too weak and dainty for carving marble, but too fat for delicate drawing. My brother learned to draw while bed ridden many years ago, as I walk in I see an unfinished mural on his wall. A woman with chocolate skin and closed eyes, Full lips and long curled hair draped around her nude body, her lips were full and smiling. She was so beautiful although unfinished the portrait took my breath away.

"Darius?" I ask softly as to not startle my dear brother, said man comes from his adjoined bathroom drying a brush with a cloth.

"You... called for me brother?" I say and he doesn't look at me, his brows furrowing, I'm worried by his sunken eyes he looks exhausted.

"Darius, have you been sleeping alright?" I ask and He laughs bitterly, placing the brush with the others.

"It's so rich to hear you say that Lynn, acting as if you care for someone other than yourself." He hasn't looked at me since I walked in,

"I forgot to Congratulate you on your upcoming nuptials." The poison dripping from his words has me flinching, his normally neat and tied back hair is unkempt and loose cascading down his shoulders.

"Y-you don't need to do that Darius but I said I was sorry for what I said to you before I feel just terrible." He interrupts me by throwing his art supplies across the room causing a loud clattering sound to ring out.

"You think I give a **damn** about a comment you made half a month ago? How **stupid** do you think I am?" He growls finally looking at me, my unease makes more sense now as he glares, the anger seething from him is so familiar to me.

"I-I don't understand Darius, I'm sorry." I say softly and he walks to me, grabbing my face tenderly.

"You don't understand? You don't understand?! How gallivanting around thinking there could be no consequences could affect those around you?" his grip tightens and I try to push him away, He grabs my arm slamming me against his door. When did he get so strong?

"You think everything is wonderful? You're getting married! You're doing what everyone wants! Do you have any idea how harmful your actions are?" my breathing picks up and my mind swims wondering what he could possibly be talking about,

"You are so **entitled,** so *selfish!* taking everything from me! You think you deserve this? You think you deserve something so wonderful?" He's pushing me so hard I can feel my skin bruising already.

"Darius you're hurting me..." I feel tears brimming in my eyes. I can't bring myself to look at his face before his hand moves from my chin to my throat.

"***Good,*** maybe you'll understand how I feel when you leave thinking you can take everything I have and everything I've ever loved with you! You're sick! You don't **deserve** to have what's going with you when you leave." I feel my airways becoming tighter as I struggle to breathe.

"You forget yourself sister. you stand below me, thinking you can just apologize for the things you do and everything will be ok? Everyone will forgive you? For being wrong and such a displeasing excuse of a Duke's daughter. You are in **MY** shadow and you should act like it instead of thinking you can do whatever you want and then leave with everything to an entirely different territory!" I gasp when he moves me, throwing my body to the ground limply. The pain and the cold from the stone steps blossoms up and through my side where I landed until it reverberates in my head causing my teeth to clamp on themselves. Luckily my tongue wasn't in the way.

"It's not a coincidence everything you do is a failure, everything you come in contact with becomes shit!" he yells at me and I feel my body shaking as I try to sit up.

"D-darius please.." I'm still so confused on why he's angry tears slipping down my cheeks, I mentally curse myself for crying again.

"You. are. Inadequacy. Incarnate." he scrunches his face at me before spitting at my feet, I can't find the strength to try and sit up farther.

"I should kill you where you stand." he huffs softly and looking up at him makes my heart stop and my blood run cold. From this angle I finally understand the familiarity of his anger as well as Herschel's. As the boy I grew up with, sick in bed stood above me. I saw my father looking back at me, His stance, and his anger which shook me to my core. The world around us went dark and I could only see him and the way his eyes burned staring at me. His words fell on deaf ears, tears streaming down my face uncontrollably, his hands were balled into fists paint splattered over his pale skin.

He walks to his wall where the mural is placing his hand on it and letting out a deep sigh, finally done yelling at me. I can see the picture closely now and for longer, delicate strokes and a familiar bed sitting under the woman that made me realize it's not just a portrait of a woman, but a still life of a girl, a real person who has been naked in my brother's bed and laughed with him, and loved him as he painted her. And Darious loved her as well. After a moment more of looking at it the girl pictured comes to fruition.

"That... that's Ophelia isn't it?" I can't stop myself before I ask and his fist clenches again. Ophelia is the maid that will leave the castle with me after I'm married meaning he won't see her anymore. I can suddenly see past his anger into the pain surging through him at the thought of losing the girl he loves. It's different from what I felt when I saw Herschel with the princess, and in that moment I knew that Darius was only angry with me because he couldn't be angry at the person who assigned her to me, our father.

"Please Linny..." He says softly, his voice breaking slightly, he doesn't look at me but only the wall.

"Go away please." his request is barely above a whisper, I stand slowly feeling my side throb an objection but walk to his door anyway. I know I should turn and hug him, tell him everything is going to be ok that I don't want... I open the door slowly to see Herschel with a worried expression on his face. It turns angry when he sees how I look before I close the door. He knows he can't do anything to my brother, he hugs me and I wince slightly. Herschel insists on taking me to my room and I let him after some insistence that I can walk there myself.

After resting for the remainder of the day as well as the following night, I am finally able to leave my room after my betrothed falls asleep next to my bedside. I could not truthfully sleep another moment even if I wanted to. Despite the well placed makeup to cover my fresh bruises I keep away from most workers as well as nobles who had overstayed their welcome in my opinion after my debut. In truth they were only around so they wouldn't have to travel back for the rushed wedding of the Duke's only daughter. People have made me more tired these days. I used to love introducing myself to strangers despite the eyerolls and scoldings I received from my mother for being too friendly and wasting time. Now the thought of talking to a stranger and telling them who I am, the people I come from sickens me to my core. I feel my heart leap to my throat when the Viscountess mentions my name talking to the other ladies of the kingdom.

"..and *I* heard he was her teacher!" She laughs and the other ladies join in, one with a particularly shrill voice speaks next.

"A regular teacher's pet isn't she? I guess we don't have to wonder how she passed so many courses with a brain like hers." Their laughter reminds me of chirping birds, squawking aloud where anyone could hear.

"I wonder how many student's he's groomed before?" They cackle to each other. I honestly wanted to tell everyone what really happened on the night of my debut but Herschel told me I couldn't. I didn't know what really happened, I could trust him, that Mr.Walsh was a monster. I felt powerless, suffocated, by what he said he gave me no choice and I'm paralyzed as the rumors grow around me like a wildfire, worse because they weren't talking about just me this time. I wonder how Sullivan must feel, most likely betrayed by me but I also wonder what if Herschel is right?

I'm snapped out of my thoughts by the yelling of my name and stomping down the hall, I turn and see my mother furious.

"Adilyn Cecelia Wardwell! Where have you been! We had an appointment yesterday and you were absent?! How are we supposed to fit you into my wedding dress if you do not show up?!" I furrow my eyebrows searching my brain for a believable excuse,

"I'm sorry mother I was... done with class and went to my room to relax for only a few moments before coming to see you and I fell asleep please forgive me." I bow to her and my words cause my mother to stop yelling if only for a moment. It's impossible to know what's going through her mind when I stand back up. She's still trying to glare at me but can't mask the confusion she has.

"I'm going to be honest I was expecting some sort of smart retort" she furrows her brows and I realize the chattering of the women around the corner has either stopped or gotten so far away that I can no longer hear it.

"Well then come with me, we have to make up for what you slept through yesterday." She grabs my arm yanking me to follow after her, I notice blood trickle down and out of my mother's nose and pull away grabbing for the Kerchief in my pocket and handing it to her.

"Mother your nose!" I warn her and she grabs it quickly placing it to her face, I can't help but be nervous at the sight.

"Are you alright?" I can't help myself before the words fall from my lips and she waves me off continuing to walk towards the drawing room.

"I'm fine darling don't worry about me" She chuckles wiping her face for the last time before placing the Kerchief into her own pocket.

"I'll return this later no worries, I only need some more medication." she suggests softly, I don't think it's a good idea but decide to not bring it up.

After we make it to the drawing room I see Archer with his fabrics and needles as well as the ugliest dress I have ever come in contact with in my life. The fabric of the top and sleeves looked like it was made of white wool, more Ideal for a mid winter wedding rather than the late summer wedding I was supposed to have. The skirt was ruffled with silk, layered like a dancers skirt until it extended way farther than it needed to. The sleeves were cinched at the end with embroidered off white butterflies dancing through the top part. The skirt was checkered with eggshell white and cream colors changing directions on each seam. The train was long and relatively simple, just looking at it made me want to physically shrivel into myself. Standing for Archer much like before my Debut I usually find the process boring, this time it's different. I feel sick, my stomach is completely normal but I feel nauseous. In the back of my throat and my chest, my mouth is dry as I stand there. I feel a flight or fight response I can't respond to and my head throbs with dizziness, I would like to go back to my room and just do nothing. My breathing picks up slightly and I try to combat my anxiety with deep breaths.

"Dearest stop it or you'll get poked." My mother says simply and I nod, I try to look through the room and see a basket by my feet. I'm not sure what it's meant for but looking in it causes intrusive thoughts to move through my head. I know I'm perfectly healthy but something about looking in the basket causes the nausea to double for only a moment and I decide if I'm going to get sick it will be there.

"I wish I could give you a dress that has more sentimental value, a family heirloom maybe, alas I was the middle child and my older sister got my mother's dress when she married, it will do to your cousin Florence when she comes of age." my mother says, suddenly snapping me out of my thoughts.

"You married... father in it, it should hold some value to you." I respond expecting my mother to agree curtly before going quiet again, I am surprised when instead she laughs quite genuinely.

"You should know more than anyone by now marriage has nothing to do with how the woman feels." she responds rather simply fanning herself while she thinks for a moment.

"The only thing really up to me was the dress and you don't even get that privilege." I audibly suck through my teeth and cringe staring at the dress half draped on my body.

"It's... wonderful mother." I lie through my teeth and my mother laughs again reaching over for her tea cup placed on the table beside her.

"I told you, you were going to get stuck." I nod, staring at my hands hearing the clink of her setting her cup again.

"So, you didn't love father?" I ask softly and my mother makes a thoughtful expression.

"I'm not sure what love is truly, at least for another person such as your father. I love this tea for instance." she pauses pursing her lips.

"I thought I knew at one time... staring at your brother for the first time I was quite overcome with something you could describe as love but," she pauses and almost seems sad.

"He was so small, so sick. I realized even the most important things could die. I tried to give your father another, stronger Heir but after you were born... the way you are-" I interrupt her without much thinking.

"You mean a girl?" I ask furrowing my brows and she nods, staring at the ceiling, not scolding me for being unlady-like and not letting her finish.

"Yes, he said he wouldn't try for another. Told me my womb was poisoned, his mistresses keep him happy now and I keep up the house. I distanced myself from him so as to not get hurt, and I distanced myself from my children even after Darius got better. Forever expecting the worst." This seems like the first real conversation I've ever had with my mother, and the glimpse I get into her life is slightly overwhelming.

"It's not as if my mother's dress would fit you anyways, she was much thinner than you." She says after a minute and I feel my head roll back and a groan rip from my throat.

After hours of standing for Archer and that terrible dress, my mother clamoring in the background how it would cost less to make me a new dress with all the fabric they're using to match it to my size. I'm finally let go, it's getting dark now the sun is still barely peeking over the horizon. As I pass by the large open windows of the dukedom, the wind blows into my face and I close my eyes taking in the smell of the late summer. I'm startled out of my thoughts at the sound of swords swinging and hitting each other, I peer down to the training grounds and see my brother in a playful sparring match with Herschel. The scene reminds me of when I used to watch them growing up, Herschel had just joined the house as a guard in training and Darius was having one of his better days, they practiced swordsmanship together as they grew older and now it was hard to tell who was better. Herschel preferred a broad sword, thick and heavy it showed as his weapon came down like a hammer when he struck. My brother was partial to a rapier, a shorter sword close to his body. It was strange to watch how the two interacted on the training grounds. I only knew so much about swords due to me reading hours of research and combat books to my brother as he layed in bed when we were children. He always said he could read them himself but I insisted, I loved it.

"My lady!" Ophilia's familiar voice calls for me and I turn to her as she bows and hands me a folded piece of paper with my name inscribed delicately on the front in large looping letters.

"My apologies for the interruption but I found this on your desk while I was tidying up your room." Ophelia explains fidgeting with her hands.

"You're fine Ophi no worries." I smile at her and her fear filled expression drops causing her to brightly smile back.

"By the way Ophilia I..." I can't help but falter slightly as her wide eyes look at me. She's such a sweet girl and she deserves the love she's found. I wish I could do something for her.

"I'm just sorry alright?" I say looking back at the window watching the sun fall and seeing a figure by the lake farther on the grounds. Ophelia's brows furrow but she ultimately decides against asking what I mean and walks away. I open the note and read through the sentences carefully, the handwriting is careful and familiar although I can not place my finger where i've seen it before.

My Lady Wardwell,

I hope this letter finds you well, for I would not wish to burden you more if you are not. I've noticed you for a long time now, I've seen your expressions change as these few weeks have transpired and to say I am concerned is an understatement. Unfortunately with your impending nuptials I am unable to speak with you in person especially due to your new upgraded guard.All i've held in for so long I can not any longer, but I do not have the willingness to face you just yet. So I would like to tell you everything I think but as to not be discovered by your beloved I will do so through a page rather than spoken word. I apologize for this inconvenience ahead of time and bid you goodbye for now.

-Forever yours.

To say getting such a letter was surprising would be an understatement, I didn't know what to do with such a letter, I was to be married in a little over a month, engaged! In love! What was this person thinking? I stuffed the letter down my dress when I hear a scream from outside, I look out the window once again to see Darious on the ground with a fatal wound bleeding on the ground, as well as Herschel kneeling next to him his discarded broad sword had a bloody tip, cast to the side as it's wielder tends to my brother.

9

Herschel had accidentally struck my brother while sparring, no one blamed him not even Darius who hadn't woken sense the incident. During the days He was recovering I had barely seen Ophilia, I expected she was most likely in the maid's quarters trying to still hide their affections for each other knowing she could not mask her fear for his life. I stayed by Darius's side the best I could but Herschel made me sleep in my own bed, this gave me the opportunity to see the many other notes hidden for me in the many places of my room, I often read them while sitting with my brother as that was the only time Herschel truly left me alone.

Week 1.

My Lady Wardwell,

You are truly the god's definition of perfection, I thought myself a man of logic over romance but knowing you has me questioning myself every day. I could be blinded and I would be satisfied only knowing I gazed upon your delicate features at least once in my insignificant life. I look inside myself and see a perilous ravine without you in my life, I hope to convince you to instead Marry me, and move to the capital then lead the life you are planning at this time.The world was once dark but I saw everything so clear after the first time you embraced me. I wish for nothing more than your forgiveness for the things people have said I've done, I am only guilty for the effect you have on me and the way you make me feel.

-Forever yours.

Herschel started standing outside of my brother's room while i'm there. He barely looked at me as I walked past him and only talked in short sentences. I assume he's wracked with guilt over the accident but things are bound to happen when boys are training together with swords.

"What am I going to do Darius?" I say softly not expecting my brother to answer, he turns a little in his sleep and I sigh.

"Herschel's changed ever since... well he's not acting like himself anymore." I used to talk with Darius on his bad days, tell him about my studies as well as mother and father. He'd sleep through it for days until he would finally roll over and tell me to shut up and let him sleep, that's how I'd always know he was going to be ok. I shuffle the three letters in my hand and find the newest one, I've only skimmed it until now.

"Something is so off about him, he either won't look at me or..." even though I knew he wasn't listening I couldn't help stopping short of the flirting Herschel had subjected me to as of late, pulling me close, kissing my skin, sniffing my hair, and then letting me go to walk away without a word. I look at the third letter in my hand,

"What do you think of this?" I ask softly looking at the letter, this one was longer than the others.

My Lady Wardwell,

I must apologize in advance for my words in this letter, I don't wish to alarm you in any way. I can not hold in my jealous feelings any longer, I saw you with him today, the knight. Watching him hold you the way I long to, the way his lips caress you makes me burn. I know there is nothing I can do and I am completely out of line but the fact I can't force your betrothed to keep his hands off you pains me to my core. I am determined to steal your heart from him. Quoting the great poet I must say to you,

"When, in disgrace with fortune and men's eyes, I all alone beweep my outcast state And trouble deaf heaven with my bootless cries And look upon myself and curse my fate, Wishing me like to one more rich in hope, Featur'd like him, like him with friends possess'd, Desiring this man's art and that man's scope, With what I most enjoy contented least; Yet in these thoughts myself almost

despising, Haply I think on thee, and then my state, Like to the lark at break of day arising From sullen earth, sings hymns at heaven's gate; For thy sweet love remember'd such wealth brings That then I scorn to change my state with kings."

I feel as if I can never say enough how I feel for you using my own words or anyone else's but I will keep trying until I find the right set of phrases to convey it properly.

-Forever yours.

I sigh deeply looking to see my brother breathing deeply and evenly as he sleeps which is a good sign.

"Whoever this man is... he wants me to marry him which means mother was wrong when she said no one would want me after what i've done." I think for a moment skimming the letters again.

"He wants to move to the capital, and live close to the academy but... the capital has more rumors than the dukedom. I don't know if I could stand living in the capital." I shake my head, sighing deeply.

"What am I saying? I'm engaged I-I love Herschel..." for a moment the room is uncomfortably quiet as I sit and wait for a response from my brother I know will never come.

Week 2.

I spend every day doing the same thing. In the morning I go to the drawing room where my mother ridicules me while my dress is fitted to me. She's decided to add a long translucent train with embroidered boars and grape vines. I could feel Archer freeze at the request before mumbling a soft prayer for me and agreeing. I am escorted to my room by Herschel afterwards where sometimes I would find a new note, and sometimes I would find nothing. Herschel escorts me to my brother's room and I talk to him, He's never been asleep for so long.

"The head house Physician is contemplating a feeding tube, you know." I tell him as I sit down on the chair that now never leaves his bedside,

"They're worried your weight will get too low if you don't eat something." I sigh deeply, taking out one of his favorite books from under the bed. He always used to leave them there for me to read to him when he was sick.

"I don't have another letter today unfortunately... I know how interesting you find them." I can't help chuckling to myself. Just as I open the book I hear footsteps and a piece of paper slips under the door,

"I may have spoken too soon." I can't help the chuckle that leaves my mouth walking to the door and picking up the paper, it has the same writing on it spelling my name out carefully.

"Curious how it was delivered here..." I trail off, unfolding the paper and skimming it, it was much shorter than I expected as well as being a Tad messier.

My Lady Wardwell,

I'm afraid my movements are being watched, and my letters could be intercepted. I will deliver my letters to this room when you are here from now on.

-Forever yours.

I flip the paper over looking for another message and am a little disappointed to find nothing. I sit back in my spot picking up the book I set down before.

"I'm sorry Darius, it was... nothing interesting." only mumbling leaves my lips, and my brother doesn't move from his slumber.

When I'm done with my brother I walk back to my room and open the door only to see it torn completely apart. Herschel is in my top dresser drawer looking frantically for something before turning around when he hears my door closed.

"Wh-what are you doing Herschel?" the words slip from my lips cautiously as if i'm speaking to a mental patient, My eyes dart towards my bed quickly. The covers are torn off and bunched up.

"You're hiding something, I know it." He huffs slamming the drawer shut and turning around, he walks towards me stomping angrily.

"I could tell by the smug face that **Bastard** gave me in the hall earlier! Where is it!?" He demands loudly and my breathing picks up, I don't know who's talking about.

"H-Herschel you're scaring me who are you talking abou-" he cuts me off by letting out an aggravated groan.

"You know who i'm talking about! Stop being so.. So stupid!" he yells turning back around and pushing everything off my desk slamming his hands down breathing heavily.

"I'll kill him! I'll kill that little..." I know I have to de-escalate this situation, I swallow hard walking closer to him.

"Don't you think if there was something to hide you would have found it?" I ask softly, reaching out a hand delicately and Herschel lets out a deep sigh.

"I-i know with the princess and now your brother you must think that I... I can't **Lose** you Adi.." He stands up, grabbing my hand and placing the tips of my fingers to his lips softly.

"I need you, i'm almost..." he trails off and my heartbeat quickens, the soft gentle boy I grew to love over the years, it was like I was finally seeing him again.

"I have to have you, Adi." He finally says with a desperate tone pulling me closer and burying his face in my neck, I can't help the chuckle that bubbles from my throat.

"You have me Herschel... I'm right here." He pulls me closer to him before moving me back towards my bed,

"No Adi I need you, right now." He lays me down almost too softly and panic sets in, it causes my blood to freeze in my veins.

"Wait wait! Herschel we're not-" He kisses me before I can finish, while reaching behind me to undo my dress.

"We're to be married anyways. What's the difference if we do this now or in a few weeks?" He tries to reason with me kissing down my neck and shoulder as my dress starts slipping. All of my courage and strength comes together to push him from on top of me grabbing my duress to keep it from slipping anymore.

"I-i'm not ready! Herschel I don't think we should do this! Please... please go away" My words get softer and my fear rings in my voice, Herschel stares down at me with a confused expression that quickly turns angry before turning and leaving my room slamming the door behind him. I slow my breathing, the letter from today barely sticking out of my dress before I take it and put it with the rest of the letters I've hidden under the mattress.

Week 3.

My Lady Wardwell,

My affections for you only grow stronger the farther we are apart, I am truly afraid of getting caught with these letters, but everyone I send brings me closer to the day I can tell you how I feel in person. I saw you through the window today, I find it amusing how your beauty can be complemented by even the most hideous of garments.I could not decide weather to feel sorry for you standing in the atrocious thing you are to walk down the aisle in, how you can even call that thing a dress i'll never know, or to feel complete awe at the way your lips moved as you spoke, the way your hair drapes down your body like a river made of the sweetest chocolate, or how your eyes still manage to sparkle in such a horrendous state of clothing. I almost can't handle watching you walk through the halls no matter how unhinged I may sound admitting it, I don't wish to do anything heinous when I see you walking the halls of the dukedom. I only crave to hold you as I have before, and see you smile again, which is something I miss dearly watching you smile even from afar. I wait to see you and let you take my breath away once more anxiously, until then,

-Forever yours.

I look up when I hear movement on my brother's bed, he's readjusting slightly and it causes him to wince, my heart races at the thought he might wake up. His face only relaxes again and I am filled with disappointment,

"I understand why you were so upset, you love Ophelia and you don't want her to leave you but..." It may be silly to choose my words carefully when I know my brother can't hear a word I'm saying but I do it anyway to try and be polite.

"I don't think there is anything I can truly do unfortunately you know how father and mother handle my opinions, although I doubt they'd listen to you either." Darious doesn't move again and I can't help letting out a sigh and opening the book on my lap to read to him.

Standing in the drawing room, I look in the mirror and see my mother's new and improved wedding dress now perfectly fitted to my body. It is even more horrifying than I thought it would be. My mother is asleep on the couch, she can't see what seems like more frills and designs then what I first thought.

"Archer... you can't possibly agree with her can you?" my mother rolls over on the couch and snores before I look back at my reflection. Archer shrugs fluttering out the skirts behind me,

"I agree with her as much as she pays me." He chuckles, his croaky voice filled with obvious sarcasm, He looks over the dress again before turning his gaze to my reflection.

"I don't love it." he admits to me standing up and kissing my cheek the way an older relative would, He smells like wood finish.

"I do believe you could make anything look good my lady." He smiles at me and my cheeks flush from embarrassment, I can't help the giggle that escapes me as he packs up his things.

"Should we wake up your mother?" He asks, after I stare at myself a little longer I look over at the duchess again, a wine glass near her head.

"I think maybe she should stop drinking with her medication." Archer chuckles while nodding in agreement and unzipping the back of my dress so I can step out of it.

"I think we should leave her where she is" Archer drapes the dress on the mannequin making a humming sound in agreement.

"She'll wake up... and figure out where we are eventually." Stepping off the stool I get dressed again and bow to Archer.

"Thank you for fitting me into... that" I can't help pausing as I gesture to what's supposed to be my wedding dress and the older man smiles at me.

"It was probably one of my most challenging works." His smile drops after a moment and I can't help but let out a snort of a laugh when he processes what he said.

"Oh! Not because of you my lady, you are..." He trails off when he notices I'm still laughing and shaking my head.

"It's fine, no worries." He starts to chuckle as well, shaking his head. I step over and move my mother's glass away from the edge of the table so it won't fall and stain the carpet.

"I'll see you another time Archer, thank you again." I smile at him again before leaving and walking to My room, a Note is taped to my door and I find it surprising that it's here and not at Darius's room, My name is scrawled across almost sloppily compared to the other notes, but I can't look at it long before hearing footsteps coming quickly down the hall. I turn around Hiding the note behind me as I see Herschel walking to me,

"Adi? You're early..." He looks confused and I'm glad I got to my door before he could, I wonder why he was coming to my room in the first place making a mental note to lock it before I leave again.

"We finished my dress, that means i'll have the free time to go back to studying." Herschel smiles his same charismatic face I recognize so clearly.

"I Can't wait to see your dress hun, but I canceled your studies indefinitely." My brows furrow at this new information and a chuckle of disbelief leaves my lips,

"That's a little extreme Herschel I mean I can find a different tutor Mr. Walsh doesn't need to-" Herschel cuts me off putting up his hands defensively,

"Oh Adi no! I just mean... we're getting married and you don't have to impress anyone because you have me and, what other reason is there for a *woman* to study?" He snickers softly at the thought mumbling about something being ridiculous under his breath. I feel my lungs expand in preparation for a deep sigh but instead turn around to open my door.

"You're right Herschel, I'll be back in a moment." I don't let him ask to come with me, closing the door before the notion can even become the fragment of an idea in his mind. I open the letter in my hand, the same handwriting as before is now messily scribbled on the page in a short note that's less than anything written to me before.

I think I've been compromised, I'll be leaving the Dukedom soon if you find this, meet me behind the caeruleum tree, in two days, under the moon.

I hide the note with the rest of them, sitting on the bed I think of who could be sending me such things but as always come up blank. My thoughts were interrupted when loud knocks shake my door,

"Are you done yet?" Herschel's voice rings out, sounding strained and almost worried despite me being gone for less than five minutes. I finally let out the sigh trapped in my chest standing up and opening the door.

"I Was thinking, we should walk around the grounds for a while." Herschel smiles but I brush him off,

"I need to check on Darius." I don't see his face change when I walk past him but I feel him grab my wrist and yank me back.

"Why the hell do you care if he lives or dies? Huh? After what he did to you?" Herchel glances down at me speaking softly, his personality completely flipped for what felt like the hundredth time this week.

"He's my brother Herschel, someone needs to look after him and god knows my parents won't." I try to pry myself from his grip but Herschel only grips my wrist harder making me hiss in pain.

"Come with me... please~ you know he doesn't give a shit about you." Herschel's begging tone moves back to harsh again fast enough to make my head spin.

"Please Adi, just spend a little time with me.. I miss you. We've been so far apart recently. I want to fix that." He pulls me closer slowly whispering in my ear,

"Darius doesn't give a shit about you... none of them do, I'm the only one you can trust, Adi please stay with me..." He begs again softly pressing his lips to my shoulder and mumbling praises against my skin, his breath is hot and inviting against me but I manage to push away.

"Herschel, if I don't care then I'm no better than they are." I wiggle out of his grip and lock my bedroom door.

"I'll see you in a few hours." I reach up to caress his face softly before walking to Darius's room to tell him about the newest note.

After two days of pacing, and going over everyone in the dukedom with my unconscious brother, I was no closer than when I received my first message.

"What am I going to do Darius do.. Do I meet them? What if it's a sick joke? Or... or an assasination attempt? I doubt anyone is going to die if I go but..." Darius moves slightly in his sleep and I walk over to feel his forehead for a temperature. He had been moving more these few days, It started with a twitch and was slowly escalating. The entire house had hope now well... the five people who knew.

"I wish you could give me advice..." A sigh leaves me when I turn away and start pacing again.

"You're Advice never helps but it does always make me laugh, you'd say something like... Linny! Just take a sword and interrogate them when you get there! Or Linny! Don't go and wear a mud mask all the time so they don't recognize you! Or-" I'm cut off by the croaky but familiar voice of my brother as he looks at me,

"Linny..." I'm instantly by his side when he calls for me I take his hand, his eyes are a bit clouded from sleep as his brows furrow.

"Darius! Yes, what do you need?" I'm prepared to get him whatever he needs, I'd sacrifice a goat in that instant if I needed to. He pulls his blankets farther up his body slowly as he turns again,

"Will you shut up? I'm trying to sleep" Darius has never been a morning person so I don't take a personal offense to his rudeness and instead run out the door to yell at the nearest maid that Darius had woken up, calling for them to get the doctor.

People were rushing in and out of Darius's room for hours and by the end of it, I was standing by the doorway watching as Ophelia held his hand sniffling as my brother talked sweetly to her. I can't help smiling at that moment and decide to leave them alone.

The sun is setting and my time to make a decision is closing, when I make it to my room the door is ripped off its hinges causing my heart to jump in my throat wondering what could have happened to make someone do this, walking to the door I see Herschel reading the notes I thought I had hidden well enough, his sword is on the bed behind him and he's scowling at the last note I received.

10

"Herschel, what are you..." I trail off when he doesn't look at me staring at the note, his brows are furrowed, and his jaw is tight, his lips pressed into a thin line.

"Who sent you these?" He speaks softly and I can barely understand what he's saying, he doesn't turn to me still so I step into the room.

"I... don't know Herschel those mean nothing I-" halfway through explaining myself he stands up taking his sword, he holds it loosely in his hand. Herschel's face is blank, unreadable his entire body loose despite his eyes being lit up like a fire,

"Don't Bullshit me Adilyn... i'm not stupid." he speaks dangerously quiet, he looks at the notes on the bed placing the last one with the others.

"Were you going to meet them? Is that where you were going?" His eyes meet mine, hot rage hidden deep behind cold, chocolate irises.

"Am I just a placeholder until something better comes along? I try so hard to..." He trails off slightly gripping his sword before raising it to sheath it again at his hip.

"I don't know who it is Herschel I swear and... And I haven't decided what I'm going to do yet." He lets out a haughty laugh after hearing me explain.

"You are so pathetic, you can't make one decision for yourself." He shakes his head before grabbing my arm at the tricep, dragging me out of the room. My muscle's throb in his iron grip trying to keep up with his fast pace.

"Herschel! Ow! Herschel you're hurting me!" I yell out but he doesn't respond until we get outside of the house. He throws me in front of him and I lose my balance falling to the ground.

"You are *my* fiancé, you are marrying *me* and now you're going to go tell whoever is giving you those notes that you. Belong. To. me. Not them, me." Herschel openly demands this taking out his sword again, causing me to wince.

"Do it or I will" he growls at me. I scramble to get up, holding my skirts up to keep myself from tripping. My breath catches walking up the hill to the large tree, I can see the carving Herschel made weeks before, thick black sap seeps from the carving bubbling down the trunk. The tree looks broken, almost tired as it stands in the sunset quickly passing below the horizon with each passing moment. I reach the precipice of the hill just as the final sun rays slip down under the horizon, the moon shines largely over the landscape and I feel as if god himself is judging me under its gaze. Looking at the pale face of it has me wanting to scream, cry, beg for forgiveness for even being born but before my transgressions can be heard a familiar voice speaks behind me.

"You look beautiful..." Sullivan Walsh compliments, he keeps a distance from me and It's understandable from how he says he's been watching me he must know that getting close can only do him harm. I'm a poison among the ones I care for, I wish to escape.

"Mr.Walsh..." His eyes light up when I address him and he steps closer to me quickly until he's close enough to offer his hand.

"Would you give me your hand My lady?" The question is something I'm not used to, Herschel puts his hands on me without much warning, the confusion causes me to place my hand in his without much thought.

"I've been fired Adilyn, I'm going back to the capital and, I had to tell you how I felt before I could go even if... Even if you didn't reciprocate my feelings." Mr. Walsh strokes my hand affectionately but doesn't take things further than that.

"I would like for you to come with me if you would be so inclined." he smiles to himself unable to look me in the face a very evident blush on his cheeks, My heartbeat quickens in my chest thumping loudly, I can't tell if i'm growing excited by the possibility of leaving with him, or scared that he will turn out like everyone else who catches any form positive feelings towards me. Before I can possibly respond to him Herschel appears out of seemingly nowhere pushing Mr.Walsh away from me.

"You bastard! I knew it was you!" Herschel yells before completely tackling the other man.

"Herschel what are you doing?" My voice rings out but I don't realize I'm the one saying it. Herschel ignores me pointing his sword at Mr.Walsh's throat so he won't struggle.

"I knew it was you, I told you to stay away from her, she's *mine.*" He completely ignores me as Mr.Walsh struggles under him.

"You don't even love her! You're just using her for your own twisted shit!" Mr.Walsh spits on Herschel from below, I feel useless watching them struggle.

Time seems to slow down exponentially, I can almost see myself outside of my body. Herschel's face changes slowly from surprised to anger, a rage I've never seen on his face. Red hot hatred moving through his expression causing his body to tense so hard he begins to shake. Herschel says something, but I can't hear it over the blood rushing in my ears. Everything is so slow, Herschel lifting his sword, Mr.Walsh's eyes widening. The moon shines on us almost blinding, it's large and causes the sky around it to be a beautiful shade of blue, The summer wind blows causing some of the last blossoms of the caeruleum tree to fall around the three of us. The dark tones of summer night compliment the dark red blood as it splatters across the ground and Herscel's uniform. My mouth is dry when Herschel stands again he doesn't look human, he sheaths his sword again wiping a mixture of sweat, blood, and spit.

"Inside, ten minuets." He demands of me before walking down the hill, the world flashes back to life. I walk to the man laying on the ground slowly in disbelief before dropping down. I didn't realize I was crying until Mr.Walsh reached up to wipe my cheek.

"Adilyn..." He says weakly, I feel a sob leave my throat as Mr.Walsh takes a shaky breath, he swallows thickly closing his eyes in a slow blink.

"Aren't... aren't you going to tell me it's okay?" I can't let out anything above a whisper as I cradle Mr.Walsh's head in my lap.

"I won't lie to you, you deserve the truth... but it's going to be okay for you at least." He chuckles and I shake my head.

"No... no I won't be okay, Mr. Walsh I'm stuck." tears drip down my face as his breathing slows and he looks tired.

"Please, i'm not your teacher anymore you can call me by my first name... you're dripping on me." I chuckle and wipe my face trying to hug him closer.

"You can't do this, you can't die, I need you." Sullivan's breathing is shallow now, he gets colder in my arms as he bleeds out.

"You don't need anyone in this place Linn..." He is whispering now he can't even say my full name.

"Please... don't... you can't." I can't seem to get anything out as I cry and he smiles chuckling.

"It's not something I can exactly stop." He moves only slightly to take my hand, gripping it softly.

"I'm so sorry" I apologize finally, reliving the way I could stop this from happening. Feeling so stupid that I only stood there like an idiot.

"Don't be..." Sullivan says, as he shakes his head and moves his hand from mine while shivering. He places it on my cheek moving my hair from my face and I reach to hold it there.

"I've wanted for almost a year... to die in your arms. Even now, I still can't help but be happy about it." He smiles softly, closing his eyes again before letting out another breath. I press his hand closer to my cheek nuzzling it slightly as the wind blows, my mouth opens to say something else but I stop, after realizing no one was listening anymore.

I hear wailing, a terrible sound filled with gut wrenching pain. I can't pinpoint where it's coming from and only realize it's me when the noise catches painfully in my throat making it crack in an ugly way. The noise quiets to a whimper until my throat is raw and I can only sob quietly. I lay Sullivan's head down slowly, my chest hurts and the wind blows. I lay down on the grass nuzzling into his chest and let him hold me the way he wished for in the letters he sent, the speedy heartbeat that used to erupt in him every time I got too close was gone now as I cry silent and steady tears. Turning to bury my face in his blood soaked shirt I inhale his scent deeply, imprinting it in my brain. Willing it to be stuck forever, the smell is sweet, mixed with spice and paper. Like a leather bound book. Eventually I can't cry anymore, I'm shaking in the night. The last thing I want to do is leave but I know it's been more than ten minutes, at any moment I'll be yanked away by Herschel. I can't get up, Herschel will never look at me the way Sullivan did, like looking at me made the world stop instead of a piece of meat to be devoured or a dog you're unsure whether to train, beat, or protect. I feel something in Sullivan's pocket reaching in and pulling out. It's a small leather bound book, I take it and hold it to my chest before sitting up slightly to finally give the first man to make me truly feel loved a soft kiss before laying back down with him again.

When I gain the strength to move back into the house, my dress is stained and my face is dirty but I can't care. My mind is completely numb with disbelief and my heart broken. I reach my room again Sullivan's book tucked neatly in my skirts, I can't bring myself to open or read it but I'll be damned if I let Herschel know it even exists. Herschel is in my room, ripping apart my textbooks, burning every letter, destroying anything Sullivan ever touched. I can't help but watch him somberly from my destroyed doorway. Everything plays like a movie and I feel as if my body isn't mine, like i'm a passenger in the back of my mind while I'm on autopilot watching Herchel breathe heavily and walk toward me when he's done.

"I'm sick of this, you're mine. From now on you do what I say." He says simply taking my hand roughly and pulling me towards him.

"You don't eat, sleep, or even *breathe* unless I say so, do you understand?" He asks through gritted teeth and I can't possibly muster anything more than an apathetic nod to him as he pulls me into the room.

"You should sleep, I'll fix your door." He sits me down on my bed, bending down and wiping dirt from my face, swiping hair behind my ear.

"I do this because I care deeply for you Ady..." He says softly, almost mumbling the words. I nod along with him, my eyes feel heavy from crying. Herschel lays me down kissing my forehead before moving the door closed and leaving me alone with my thoughts. I don't feel tired, I don't feel anything, I don't want to be alone. Even if Herschel was screaming at me I wouldn't have to think, I wouldn't have to relive watching the life drain from Sullivan Walsh's eyes quite so often.

I don't sleep, I don't clean up, I only lay staring at the wall as the world goes on around me. Herschel tells me I shouldn't leave, that he was the only one I needed. I didn't know how long it had been, hours, days, weeks. I don't feel it if I'm hungry, I don't feel it if I need to use the bathroom, no one except Herschel comes to my room. I watch over and over as Sullivan dies in my head and I do nothing, I can't believe I did nothing.

The next time Herschel comes to my room he stares down at me,

"I realize I scared you the other day but you have to get up, you stink." Herschel is smiling, like nothing happened. Where is Sullivan's body now? Probably in an unmarked grave somewhere he doesn't deserve, I felt like I needed Herschel because no one else would have me, But Sullivan's words had been ringing in my head his entire last moments had been replayed hundreds of times.

"Why did you..." My voice comes out strained, it cracks and I try to swallow so I can speak properly.

"What?" Herschel asks, making me sit up holding me upright, I feel his fingers on my dress taking me out of it. A glass of water catches my eye on the nightstand, its freshness is evident by the condensation on the cup. I take the glass holding it in my hand for a moment, the clear liquid swirls around.

"I brought that for you, I figured you'd be thirsty." Herschel chuckles as I take a sip,

"Why did you do that to him?" My voice is steadier than I expected it to be, I can't look at Herschel without seeing how angry he was at that moment. He chuckles as the dress slips off my shoulders, He cups my chin and makes me look at him with a gentle smile.

"I couldn't have you running away with him and ruining my big plans." he kisses my forehead before standing up to look in my closet, this Is my first time naked in front of Herschel and I can't help but feel so exposed despite him not planning on doing anything dastardly.

"He was leaving, why couldn't you just let him?" The question tumbles from me before I could stop it tears burning when I hear him laugh again.

"Well I couldn't take the chance dearest," Dearest, all the people calling me honey, dearest, when the only thing dearest to them has nothing to do with me.

"I wouldn't have gone, not with him and I don't want to go with you either." Sullivan's words rage in my memory, anger flowing through me, pulsing from my heart and brain to the tips of every appendage. It gets hotter, more intense when Herschel laughs louder once again.

"You don't really have a choice, Adi." Standing I snach a dress from him, a sea foam green dress with gold accents. It almost rips from my anger when I slip it on,

"Don't 'Adi' me, I have a choice! I'm human after all! I don't need you! I don't need anyone!" Herschel's face is more apathetic than shocked, he watches me closely, moving from one end of the room to the other gathering my things.

"I refuse to be a Ghost of myself anymore, a Zombie who can't stop people like *you*." my breathing is heavy from suddenly using so much energy after being sedentary for so long.

"I have done so much... to make everyone around me approve of me and I'm **done**! None of you are *ever* happy when is it *finally* my turn? Don't I get to be happy? Starting now... I'm doing things for *myself* including leaving this hell hole **alone** Herschel Stott I won't ma-" halfway through my indulgent rant I am completely cut off by a familiar broadsword to my throat and a grim look in Herschel's eye.

"You think I care if you don't want to marry me? Adi~" He coos softly, dangerously, using my pet name against me, he walks around my body, slow steps, deliberate, until the edge of his sword is placed snugly under my chin.

"True you aren't repulsive to look at... but *Darling* you're not rather compelling either." He finally speaks frankly with me, combing his fingers through my hair absentmindedly.

"I need you Adilyn... but not in a possessive loving way, i've achieved minimum power being knighted, I want *more* marrying you will earn me the title of count. Then someday perhaps **Duke** with the right attitude towards your father, we both know he favors me more~" His touch shifts from light to possessive again when he pulls my head back to look at him.

"Oh but I still won't marry you and you won't get what you want." The high pitched mockery of my voice rings out as he walks around me,

"These statements are true, however if you refuse me... you'll have no choice but to watch as I finish what i've started with Dear brother Darious, and who would believe you after you yourself said that teacher touched you in those ways. And after I caught him trying to do it again to my dear Adilyn who I 'Love So Much'" He puts the words in quotes rolling his eyes and making his true nature as well as his feelings abundantly clear.

"No one blamed me for Killing that old Pervert." He laughs darkly, seeming to be genuinely amused. He had trapped me, I had no way out, tears slipped down my cheeks as the realization became me.

"Fuck..." I swear softly, dropping to my knees and hugging myself. The man I used to Love, Herschel Stott, the simple boy I grew up with was in truth a sadistic bastard and that fact alone broke my heart and mind. Herschel stands up slowly,

"I can't watch this... you're so ugly when you cry. I'm moving up the wedding, be ready in a week." He leaves without a proper goodbye, just cold truths as I hold myself. It's my fault and I knew it, I should have seen the signs of the manipulation. I knew what Sullivan was, but I didn't speak up and now everyone in the Dukedom believed Sullivan was a Rapist, and no one will know who he truly was.

Sullivan Walsh was a wonderful man, who was sweet and handsome. Sullivan was twenty nine. Before he died, even if he still did it just for me, Sullivan Walsh hated teaching.

11

Due to the rain all week, the wedding of the year was set to be inside. I stood one final time with my mother in the drawing room, a maid does up my wedding dress as she paces.

"That *boy*..." Her face is in a misleading scowl as she talks about Herschel.

"I can't believe that boy! How wonderful he is!" She exclaims, suddenly moving the maid out of the way to work on my corset herself.

"What could have happened?! If he hadn't struck down that terrible man!" she pulls the corset too tight around me but my mind is too drunk on sadness to notice the dull throbbing in my lungs.

"Goodness! Have you put on weight? I could have sworn you were thinner than this" My mother doesn't speak directly to me, more about me and I shrug in response. I haven't paid much attention to my weight in the last few weeks that I've admittedly spent doing more sulking than exercise.

"Hopefully Herschel won't turn you down seeing this, you truly are lucky..." she's silent for a moment, looking me over almost somberly.

"You know he's too good for you Adilyn, yes?" She wipes her skirts off sitting on the couch and picking up her wine glass. Rain hammers outside on the windows, my gaze flickers to the floor then back up at her.

"That's a rather hurtful remark mother..." My voice comes out small and child-like, the fact my mother could possibly think so low of me causes my heart to hurt.

"The corset is too tight, am I... am I to breathe?" I try to complain but simply can't find the strength to speak too much out of turn anymore.

"Darling I'm only kidding, you're too sensitive." she waves me off and I grit my teeth to keep from spitting insults back at her.

"Can I be alone mother?" my voice is just above a whisper, I watch her finish her wine with a final gulp and stand.

"Of course darling, I'm sure you need a moment to reflect before the happiest day of your life." After a moment I heard the door close, and let all the air I was holding in my body leave in a deep sigh. Looking in the mirror I can't decide if I'm more disgusted by the wedding dress on my body, or the body inside it. After hours of painful hair pulling, a heavy powdered wig set on my head. It's itchy, and the light color clashes with the cream of the hideous wedding dress.

"What kind of a god would make me look so..." I trail off before I'm interrupted by the door opening again.

"Jesus Linny... what did they do to you?" I recognize Darius's voice before I turn around to see him, I can't help the smile that creeps on my lips.

"Is it truly that bad?" I ask Darius, he chuckles and pulls me into a hug, stroking my back slowly.

"Dear little sister... I'm so sorry for how I treated you, I let my anger get away from me." He whispers apologies to me, and I tell him I understand hugging him back.

"Our lives aren't the easiest brother, we're allowed to lose our temper." Darius chuckles, He looks so handsome in his fanciest outfit, A frilled collar and fresh shaven face, although he was holding his side where his injury is as he stood. "If I had one wish to change about my wedding, I would change my maid just for you." I can't help letting out another deep sigh before Darious hugs me again.

"Oh! My sweet little sister! I know it may not be what you always dreamed of but... you look more beautiful than any other girl could in that dress." He takes my hands and kisses my forehead causing me to blush and wave him off me with a giggle.

"You forget yourself Darious!" I can't remember the last time I connected with my brother this way, it felt so refreshing to have someone I can be at ease with again.

"I wanted to thank you for sticking by my side when I was hurt... I wanted to tell you after the ceremony today..." He steps back from me with a nervous expression.

"I'm going to the Amore district to study Painting, it's the most romantic place in the country with the best artists around." He shrugs and I look up at him, confusion blossoming through me.

"What... What of Ophelia?" My voice is more panicked then I mean it to be, Darious lets out a sad sigh.

"I'll leave her in your care Linny... make sure she's happy." He hugs me again to hide his expression, and I return the embrace.

After Darious left it was time to put on my face, maids gather around and slather a paste-like substance on my skin, probably lead based. I stare at my reflection looking like a ghost under the substance.

"Is nothing natural about a wedding?" I can't help asking before my face is pulled from my line of sight.

"I believe the flowers are real, My Lady." Ophelia says quickly, she doesn't seem sad, only distant and not as bright as her usual self. I can't help laughing at her comment anyways before my cheeks are grabbed. Her fingers squeeze my face and force my lips to purse so she can paint a deep red color onto them.

"Charles! I need the powder!" one of the other maids calls out, after another moment a plush pillow is thrusted into my face without warning. I cough, turning my head away as the maid yells out again.

"Charles! More powder!" This process repeats a few more times before Ophelia and I are both coughing.

"Jesus! That's enough! Now I have to start over..." She huffs softly before grabbing my cheeks again.

After my makeup is finished, people start filing out again. I grab Ophelia's elbow, keeping her behind.

"Ophi... I'm so sorry, if I could do something you know I would. I mean, are you ok?" Ophelia's face is shocked. Unlike the usual smile that would grace her lips, her face is sad.

"My dear Lady Adilyn" she takes my hands in hers before clasping them together.

"You are truly the sweetest person i've ever met, you deserve this happiness, you deserve everything you get today." I'm sure her words are meant to be positive and cheerful but I truly don't know what I will be getting today.

"Ophilia, I'm glad I'll have you with me at least." tears sting at my eyes when i'm finally alone again but I know crying will only ruin all the hard work on my face the maids did.

Standing behind the closed doors before the massive ballroom, I hear rain patter on the large windows before thunder claps, it seems to shake the entire house as maids fluff my dress. I feel dizzy when I think of all the decisions that got me to this moment. I feel so pathetic trying to get approval from people who don't care about me but I've never been able to stop myself.

"When will my father be here?" I ask a slender and almost wiery girl as she tries to move bright red flyaways out from her face.

"The Lord is already at the altar My lady." She speaks quickly and places the veil on my head adding another weight to the powdered wig held in place by a mass of pins on my head.

"Yes but when will he be back here to walk me down the aisle?" I can't help the bitter tone that codes my words, getting annoyed that I have to ask again. The girls look at eachother, the red headed girl wipes sweat off her hands onto the front of her uniform, the blue cloth of her pants showing she's not the lowest level of maid but definitely not a head maid so she does know.

"He... He's staying with the groom, you're walking the aisle yourself my lady" She says hesitantly, a lump grows in my throat and I don't even know why I care about what he thinks or how he treats me but I still wanted him there for me.

"I'm so…" I trail off before the words can fully leave my mouth, I feel stupid, standing there with all these people I don't even know fussing over a dress I despise.

"Fine. I'm sooooo fine." I punctuate my words by pulling my dress away from the many hands behind me.

"Jesus believe me it will never be good enough so just stop!" I can't help but yell at the girls, falling into the habits of the rest of my family.

"Let's get this over with" I let out a deep, almost sad breath before the doors were finally opened.

12

I wasn't nearly as nervous as I imagined I'd be as I slowly walked to my husband to be. The music was something I didn't recognize and much too cheery for what I was feeling, I wondered if maybe the minor key version would be played at my funeral or if when I died anyone would care. My heart was heavy as I saw Herschel, the boy I used to adore, now I only wished for Sullivan to be at the end of what seemed like a never ending journey to the altar. Herschel has a charming grin on his face but it feels more mocking. The world is painted gray from the storm wailing outside the large windows of the houses farthest northern ballroom. The lake thrashes far below us, small licks of water quickly turning into thrashing and vengeful waves. I don't hear the priest start, my thoughts swirling once again with Sullivan's final moments. I know what Herschel did, I know what he tried to do to my brother but not why I didn't speak up, I felt like I was drowning every moment of my life. Moments where I believed Herschel, his heart steady when he confessed to me, where even being close to me made Sullivan's heart double its pace. It made my own chest ache. The world was so slow, I looked down at the ring on my finger feeling my breath quicken, where did he even get this ring? I look at the audience, hundreds of people dressed in the peek of fashion. They seem uncaring, almost bored. My father sips a glass of a clear liquid, while my mother sniffs something off one of her long painted nails. This was my home, a mother and father who never cared and were often inebriated, a man who has been conning me since childhood, a brother who could die from a cold. I have been tortured but I am not innocent, I could have seen all of this coming if only I was a little bit brighter.

I hear my name called and look at Herschel, he's glaring dangerously at me although his smiling face still stays the same.

"Do you, Miss Adilyn Wardwell, Take Herschel Fredrick Stott to be you-" The priest doesn't get to finish before the word slips from my lips.

"No!" A confused expression washes over Herschel's face as well as the priest before I step back, I didn't know Herschel was holding my hands before I felt them slip away. Sullivan's words ring through my brain again and I hear them as if he stands beside me.

"No I don't need this... I don't want this, I don't need you." Finally speaking my mind causes a tremendous weight to lift from my shoulders. I couldn't tell anyone the things Herschel did because no one would ever believe me, and I don't need them to. I hear Herschel take a step towards me causing my mind to flash back to reality, He is no longer smiling.

"Don't!" I call to him putting my hand up, to my surprise he stops where he is.

"Adilyn, this is ridiculous! you just have some cold feet, we love each other remember?" Herschel's words are calming but his eyes are dangerous.

"No Herschel I... I used to love you but the things you've done to me I can't forgive." It's my father who speaks up now standing and throwing his glass to the floor.

"Damn it Adilyn! stop being so selfish! You threw your chance for options away!" I swallow hard not having the strength to stand up to my father.

"I used to love you, You made me feel things. My god I felt so lonely before you but I... I loved you so much I completely forgot what Hating myself even felt like." Herschel gets fed up with my words moving forward and grabbing my wrist causing me to hiss in pain.

"You could do a lot worse, you know? The next man you manage to land could beat you for such rudeness." He doesn't yell surprisingly, I try to pull away from him as he continues.

"You don't get a choice, you were promised to me, you're *mine* and if I have to kill a thousand perverted scholars to have you I will." His grip gets tighter with each passing second despite his voice saying even.

"Because you don't beat me doesn't make you husband material Herschel that's the bare minimum!" I can't help yelling at him trying to pull my arm away from him, feeling the dress rip slightly as I move.

"Adilyn, your gown be careful!" my mother yells not caring about the person inside of it.

"Stop acting like a child and get back to the altar Adilyn!" My father yells and I feel tears prick my eyes.

"You don't even care about how I feel! You don't care about what he has done father?!" I yell again as Herschel yanks my arm again.

"Admit what you did Herschel! Admit it and I'll marry you!" I don't know the reason for my insistence, they'll never listen to me.

"He's a hero! You're crazy!" my father yells, another yank of my arm follows, it's starting to feel painful.

"We can get you help after the ceremony Adi..." Herschel coos softly and I close my eyes tightly.

"Don't try to gaslight me! I Know what I'm saying!" My head is spinning. I can't keep anything I feel inside myself any longer, it's all come to a boiling point. I can't watch myself stand at a crossroads and stay speechless any longer, watching my actions take me down a path of destruction. I need to try and be better, to not believe what everyone says, I need to not be stupid.

"I know that i'm right so I will stand here and tell you I don't deserve what you've done to me! What any of you have done, I will *make you hear me* or die trying." Before anyone can react I pull again just as a thunderclap and a bolt of lightning flash startling everyone in the room. I pull too hard, slipping out of Herschel's grip and ripping the wedding dress in the process. I try to catch my footing by walking backwards quickly, this action causes me to trip even farther on my veil before falling into the large window behind me, as I crash through the glass I feel pain from the impact blossom through my back. The air is forced from my lungs for a second leaving me truly breathless, pinpricks erupt on my skin coupled by rain drops from the glass cutting my skin and the pouring rain. I see my veil fluttering above me while I fall, then warm tears float from my cheeks to the air. I don't feel scared, I feel sad knowing the last seconds are upon me and I had nothing with my life, this is not what Sullivan had told me to do. I feel slightly like I'm flying. The broken window looks like diamonds, once again the world is in slow motion and I am left to ponder if I could fix the things that had gone wrong in my life, I didn't want this. My head turns to the side, I see the hill my tree sits on. The thunderclap and lightning had struck it splitting it in half, it was still smoking. I couldn't help watching It as I felt myself drift down, the rain was so cold, the tree looked so sick, I felt so tired, I didn't want to die.

When I hit the water I feel pain blossom from my back again and ignite every nerve in my body. The automatic gasp fills my lungs with water, the dress wrapping my body was so heavy it dragged me down but I wouldn't be able to swim due to the amount of pain moving through me. My lungs burned as they filled with water causing me to let out a silent scream that only invited more liquid into my system. I was suffering and thrashing wildly and as I cried, I thought of Herschel's smug face looking at me, I thought of my father screaming, my mother's undermining words, I thought of my brother laying in bed sick and dying, and I thought of Sullivan, his cold body somewhere unknown to me and how I would join him soon in a much less peaceful way. I hated them. I hated everyone who led me to this much suffering and soon I was screaming for a different reason. I needed to hate the world at that moment as tears still slipped from my eyes and into the inky abyss around me. As I screamed something wrapped around me, I couldn't see it but it was large and gentle, it pulled me slowly until I felt rain on my face again. I could see the sky and I coughed breathing air for only a second before water erupted from my insides, the thing was still around me and as I looked down it seemed almost like a very large hand. After a moment I was on the other side of the lake, a place I've never been, and set down on a beach. Before I could react much farther, my body felt heavy and cold. I shook hard even as my vision faded in and out of blurs of color, my heart pounded hard in my chest until I couldn't hold my head up any longer. I felt the rain on my back, and the sand on my cheek before my eyes closed and I drifted into a deep unknowing sleep.

Part 1 Fin~

9 7 9 8 2 1 5 1 2 4 3 4 5